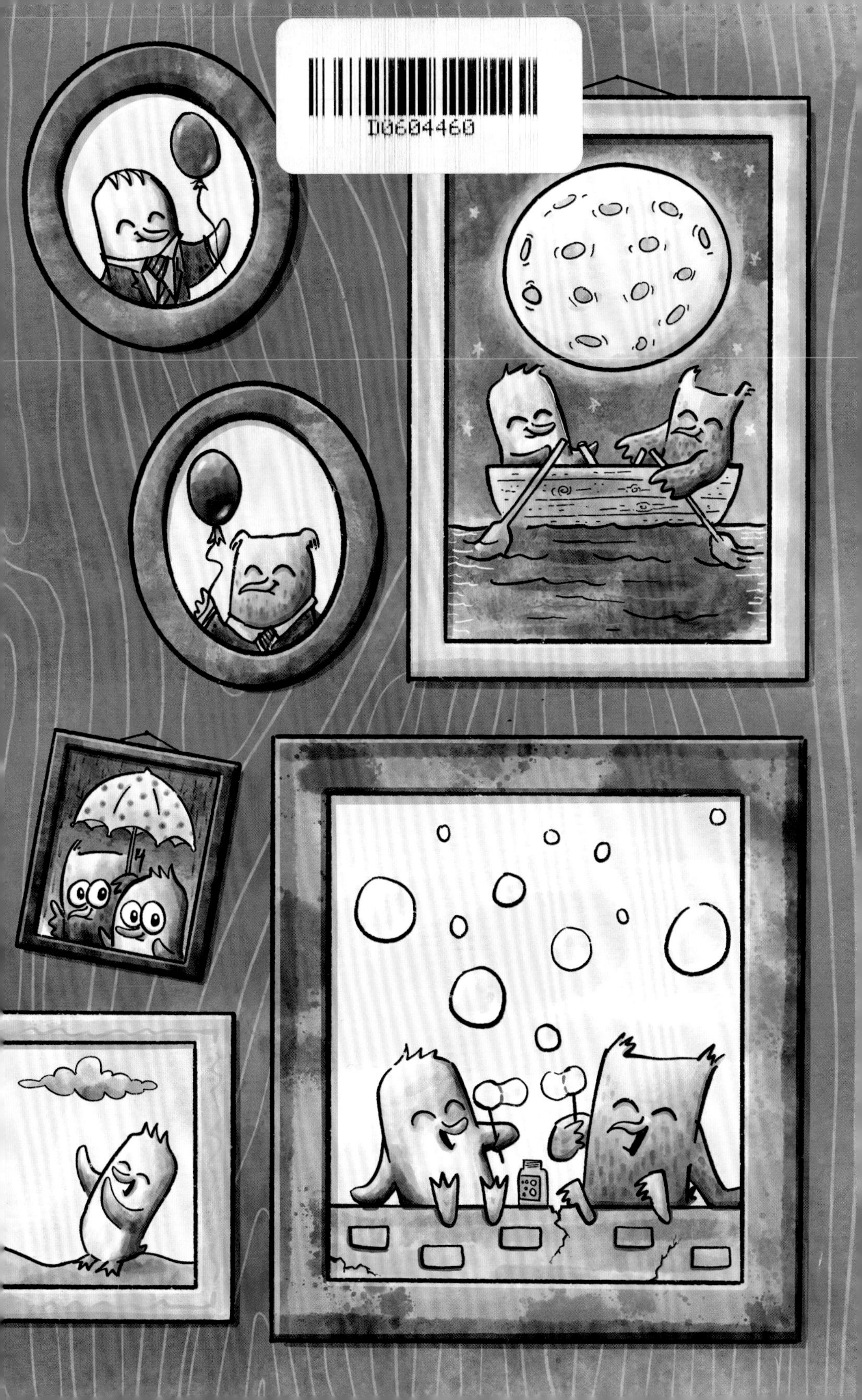

For Prithvi

Special thanks to the Tighty Writies (Allyson, Curtis, Dan, Dana, Dori, Jeanie, Kevan, Laurie, Lisa, and Lois).

Copyright © 2022 by Vikram Madan
All Rights Reserved
HOLIDAY HOUSE is registered in the U.S. Patent and Trademark Office.
Printed and bound in May 2022 at C&C Offset, Shenzhen, China.
The artwork was hand drawn on a tablet computer.
www.holidayhouse.com
First Edition
1 3 5 7 9 10 8 6 4 2

Library of Congress Cataloging-in-Publication Data

Names: Madan, Vikram, author.
Title: Owl and Penguin / by Vikram Madan.
Description: First edition. | New York : Holiday House, [2022]
Series: I like to read comics | Audience: Ages 4-8. | Summary: Despite their
differences, two unlikely friends flock together like birds of a feather.
Identifiers: LCCN 2021059791 | ISBN 9780823451500 (hardcover)
Subjects: CYAC: Graphic novels. | Owls—Fiction. | Penguins—Fiction.
Friendship—Fiction. | LCGFT: Graphic novels. | Animal fiction.
Classification: LCC PZ7.7.M3318 Ow 2022 | DDC 741.5/973—dc23/eng/20220310
LC record available at https://lccn.loc.gov/2021059791

ISBN: 978-0-8234-5150-0 (Hardcover)

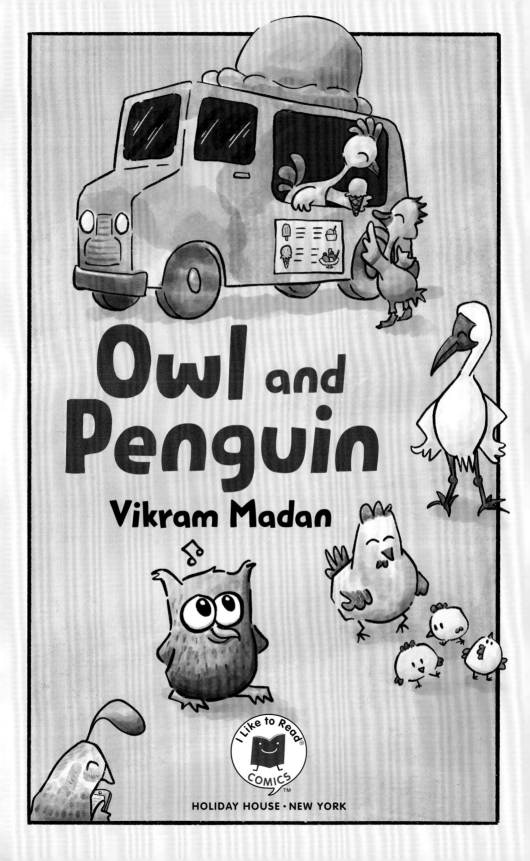

Owl and Penguin

Vikram Madan

I Like to Read® COMICS ™

HOLIDAY HOUSE · NEW YORK

ICE CREAM

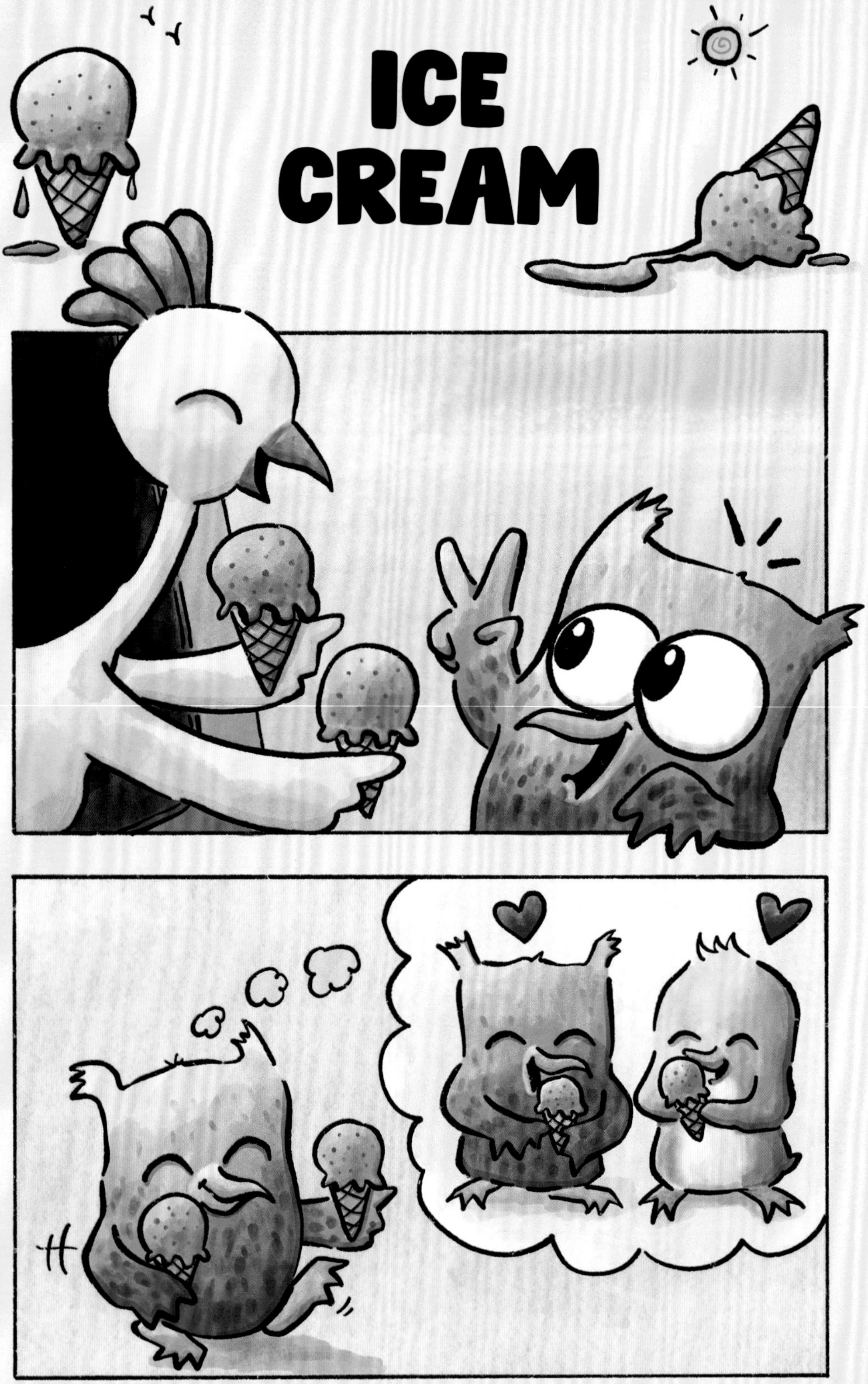

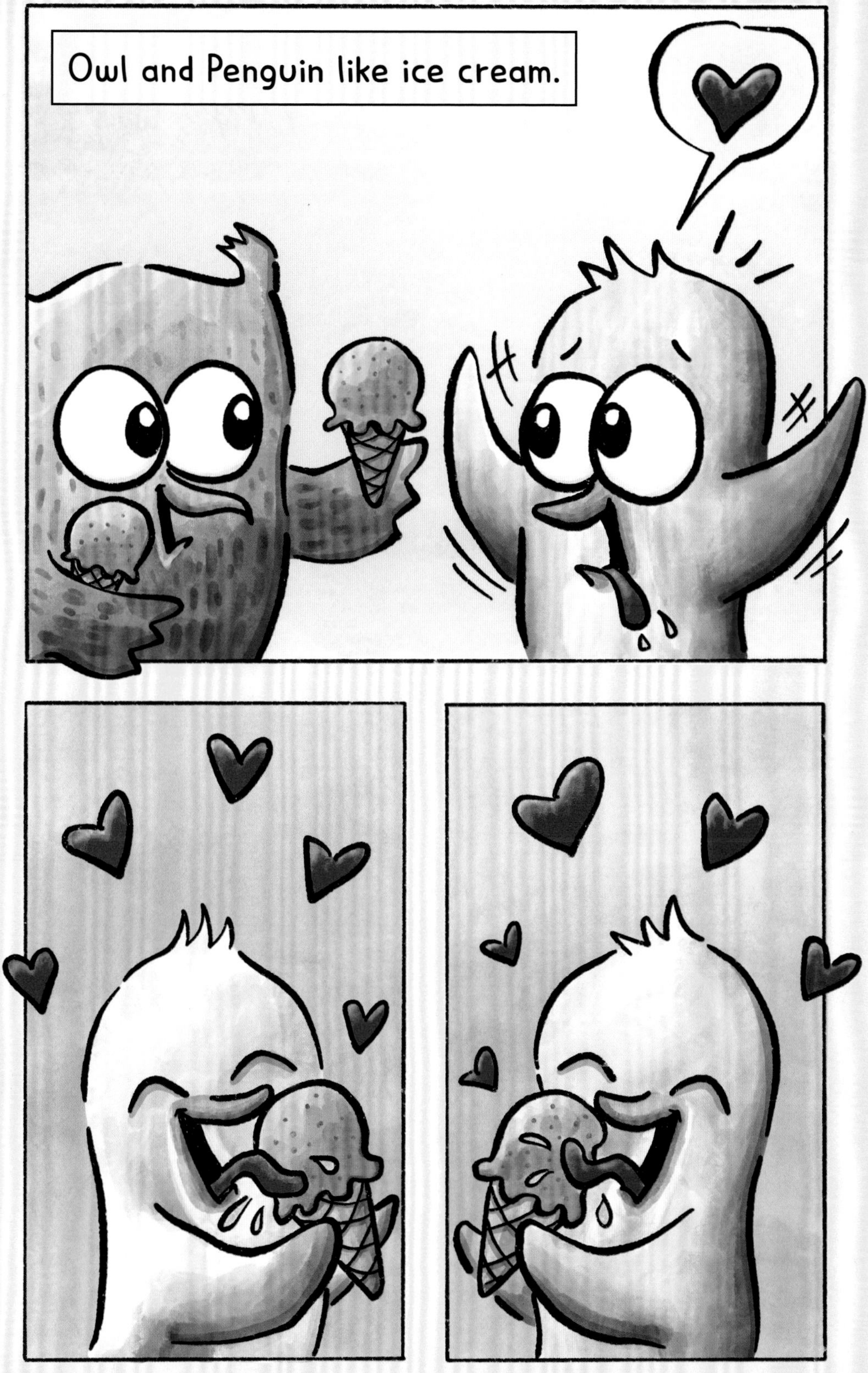
Owl and Penguin like ice cream.

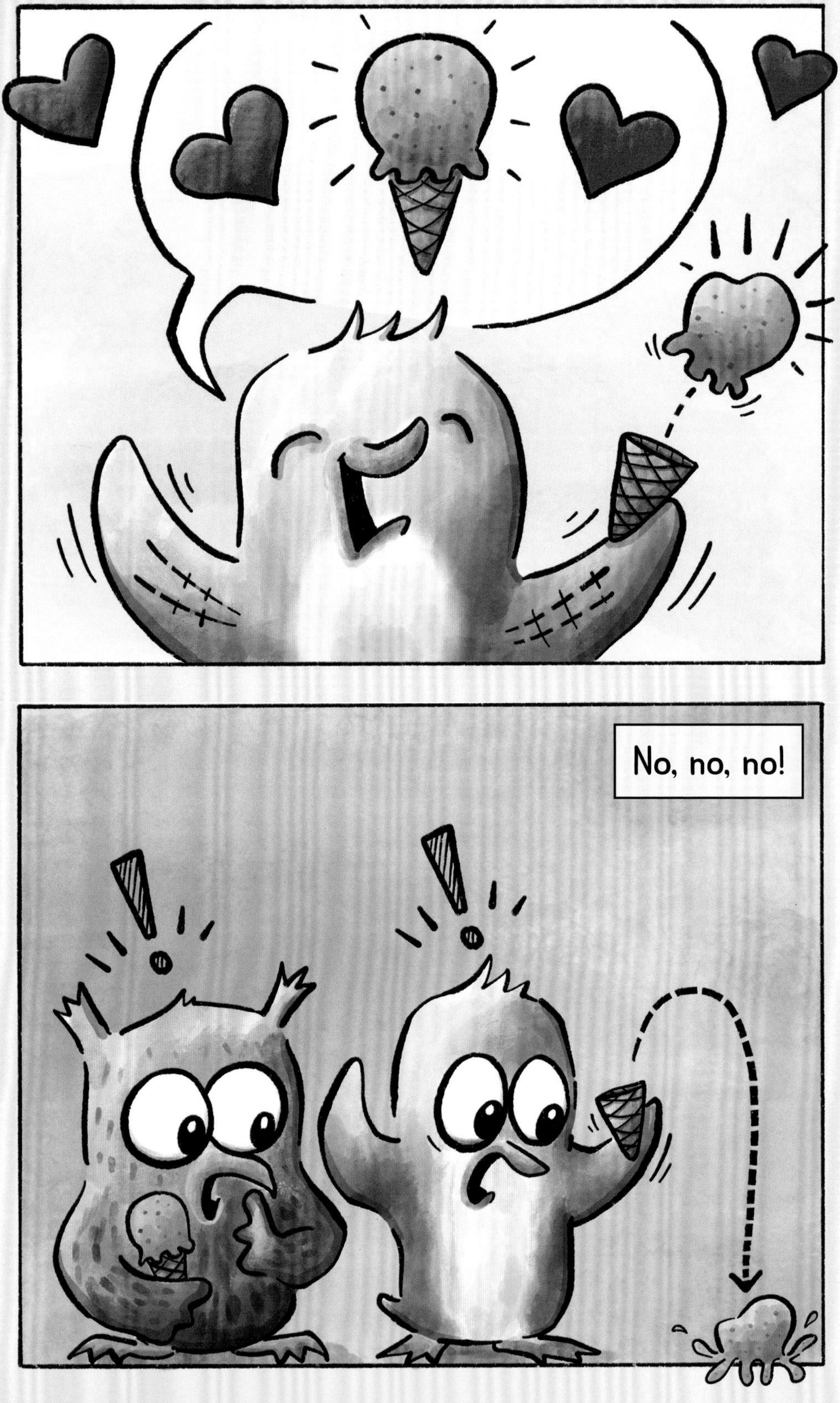
No, no, no!

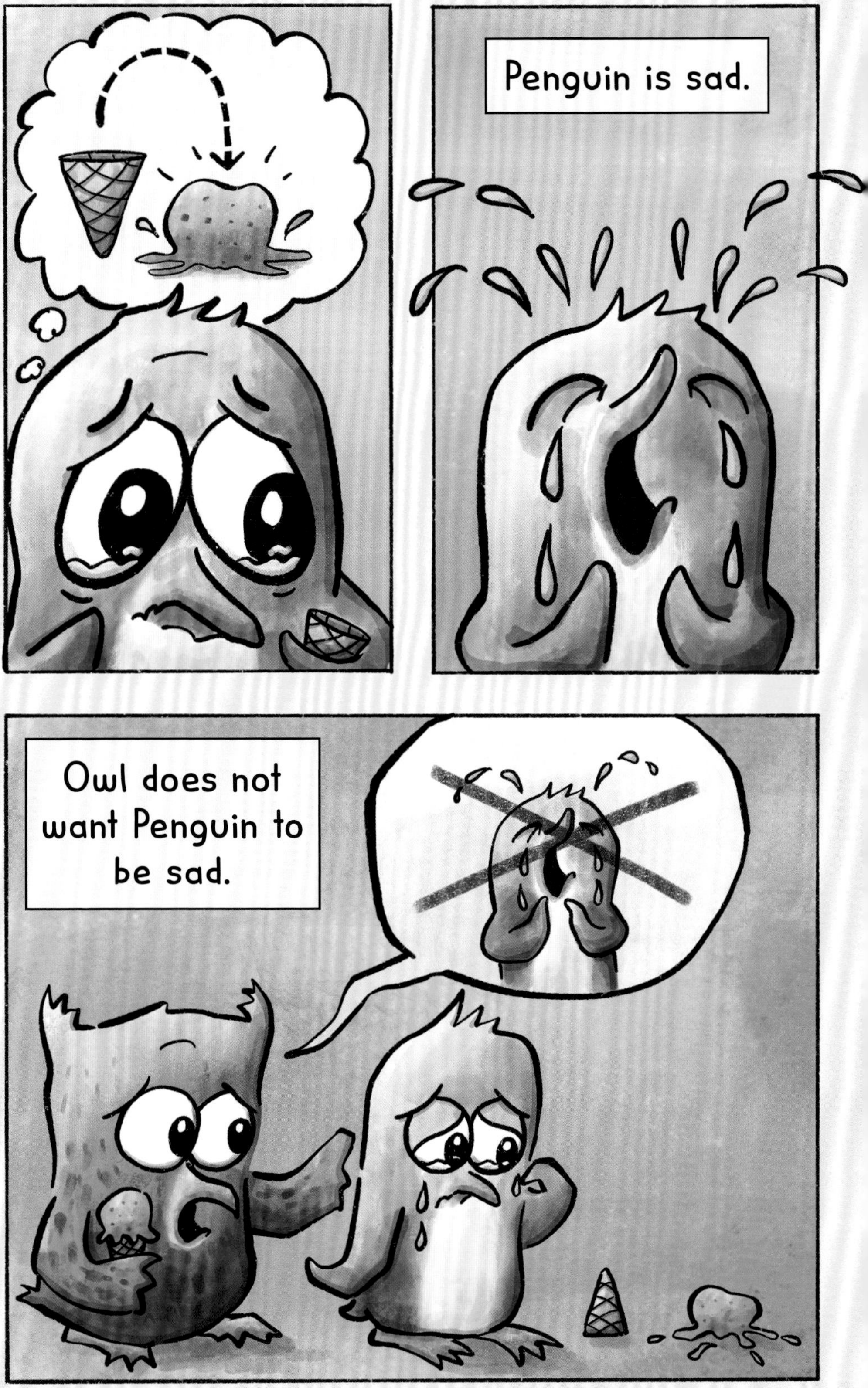
Penguin is sad.
Owl does not want Penguin to be sad.

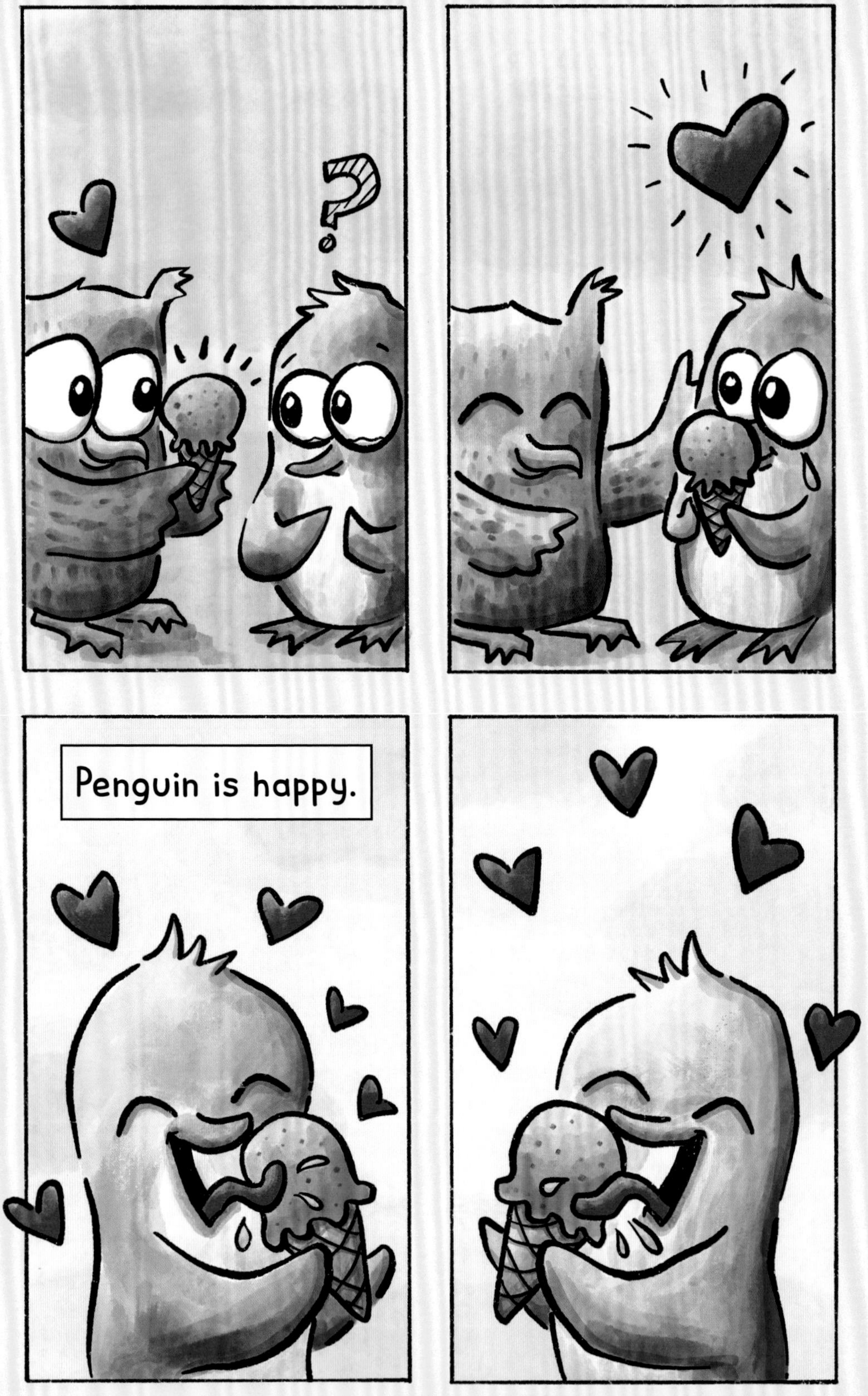
Penguin is happy.

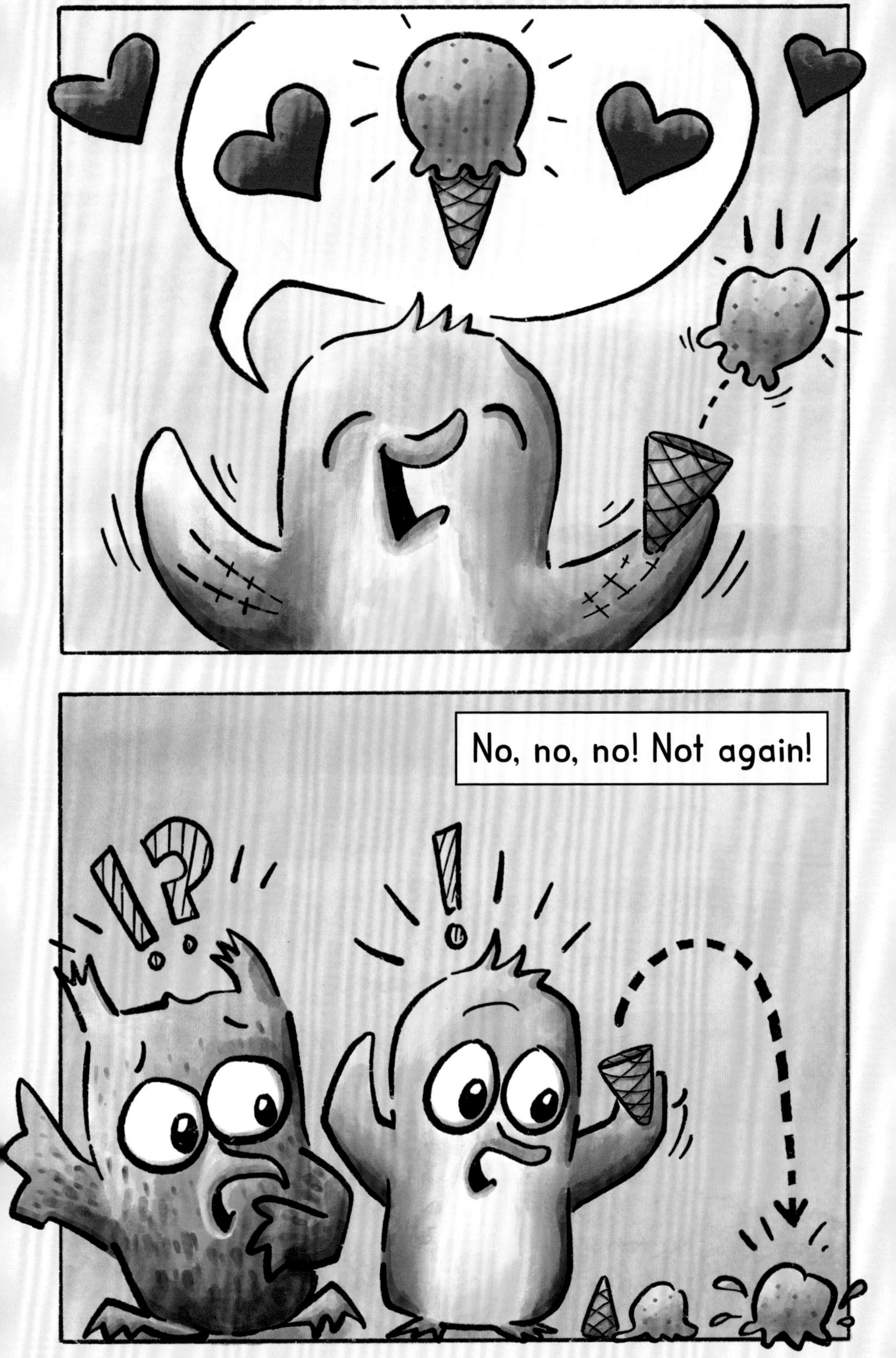
No, no, no! Not again!

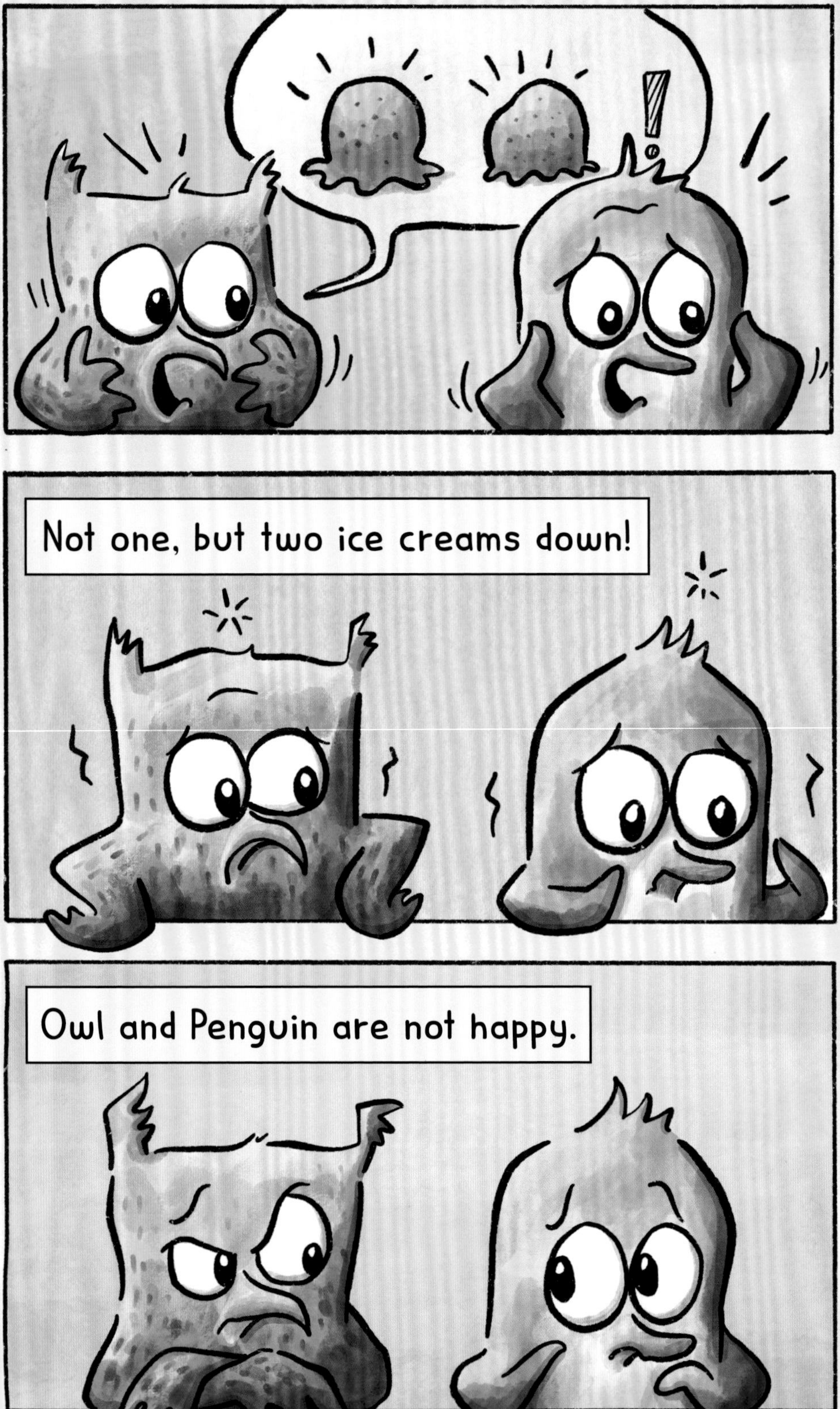
!
Not one, but two ice creams down!
Owl and Penguin are not happy.

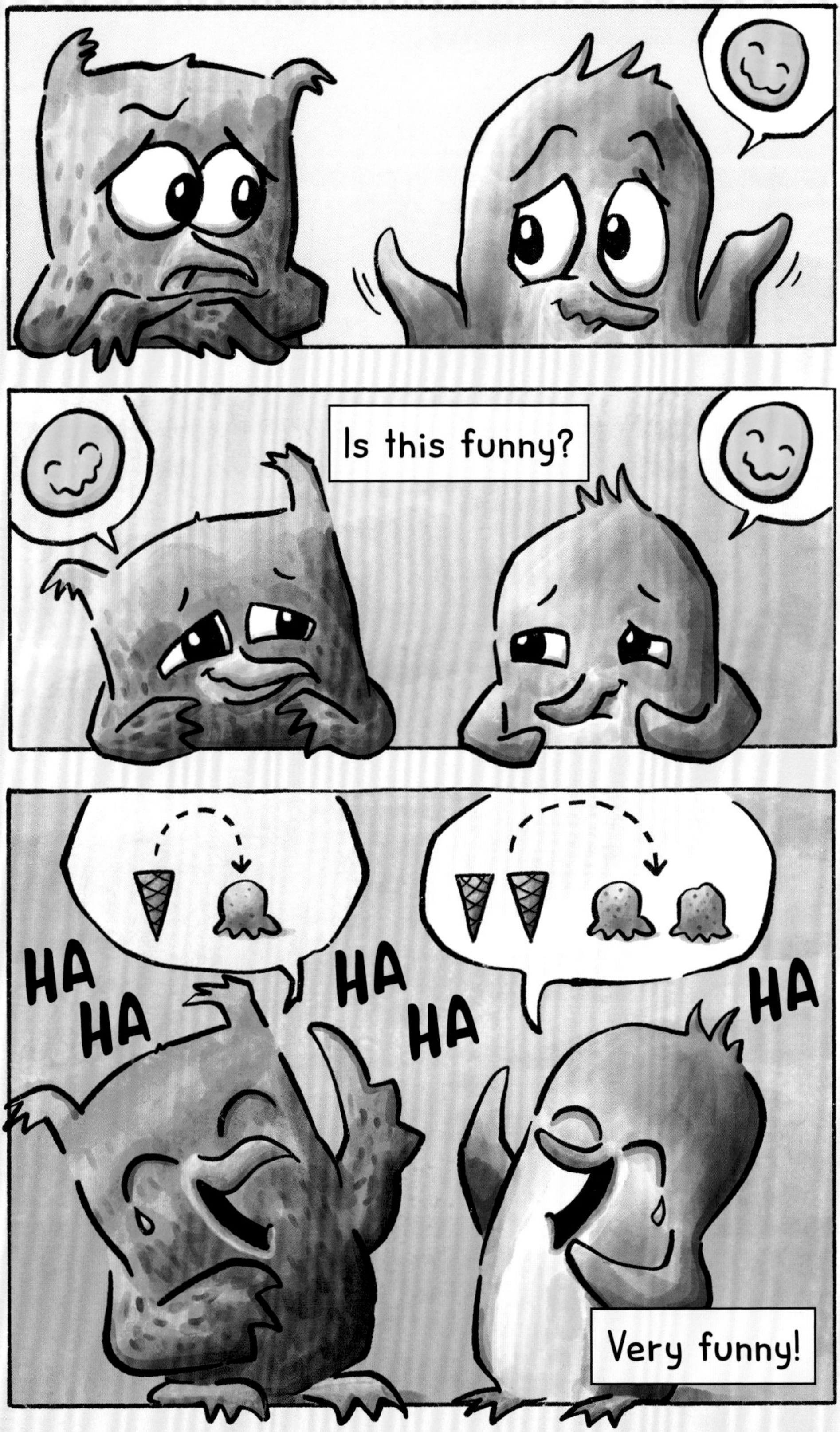
Is this funny?
HA
HA
HA
HA
HA
Very funny!

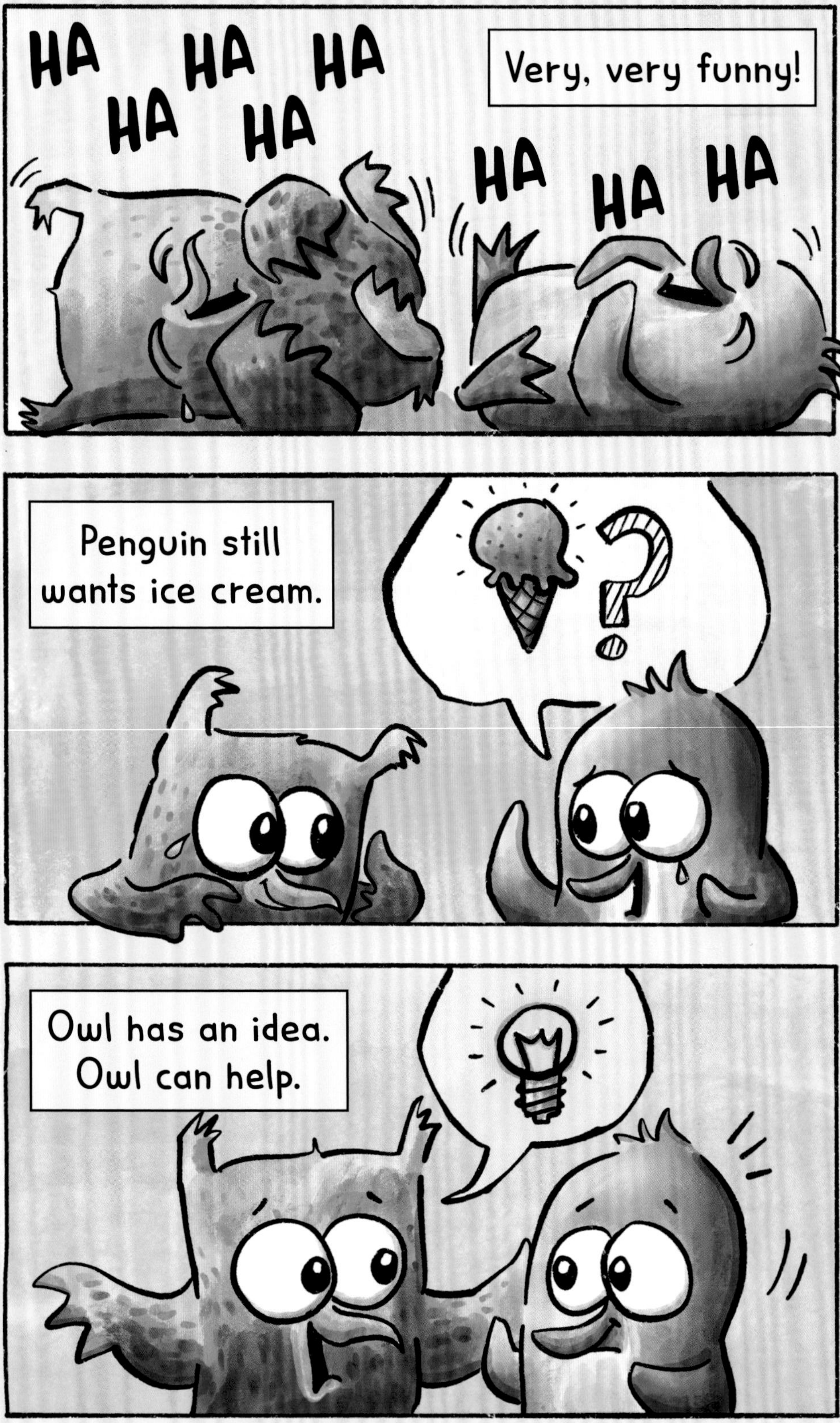
HA HA HA HA HA
Very, very funny!
HA HA HA
Penguin still wants ice cream.
Owl has an idea. Owl can help.

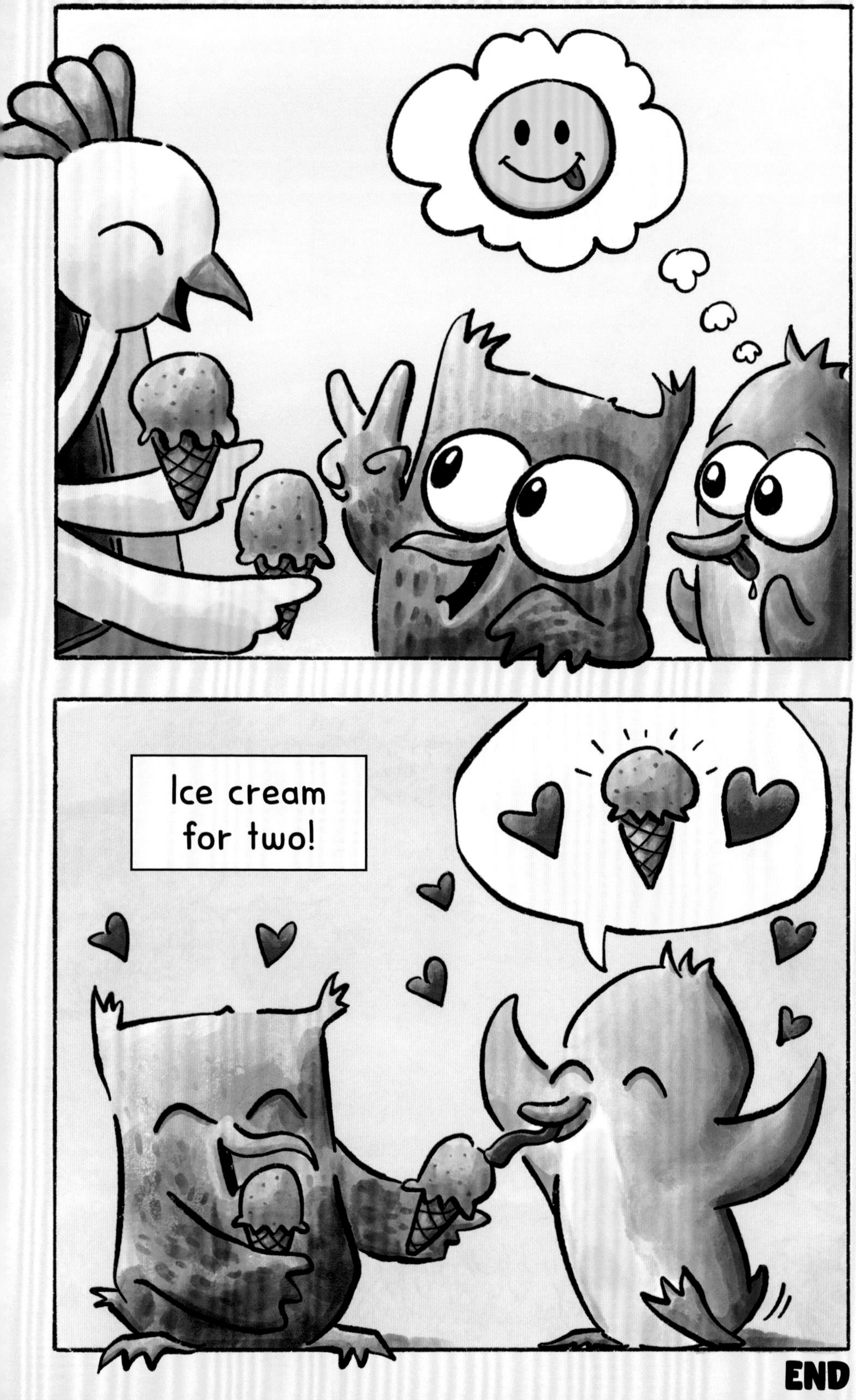
Ice cream for two!
END

FLYING

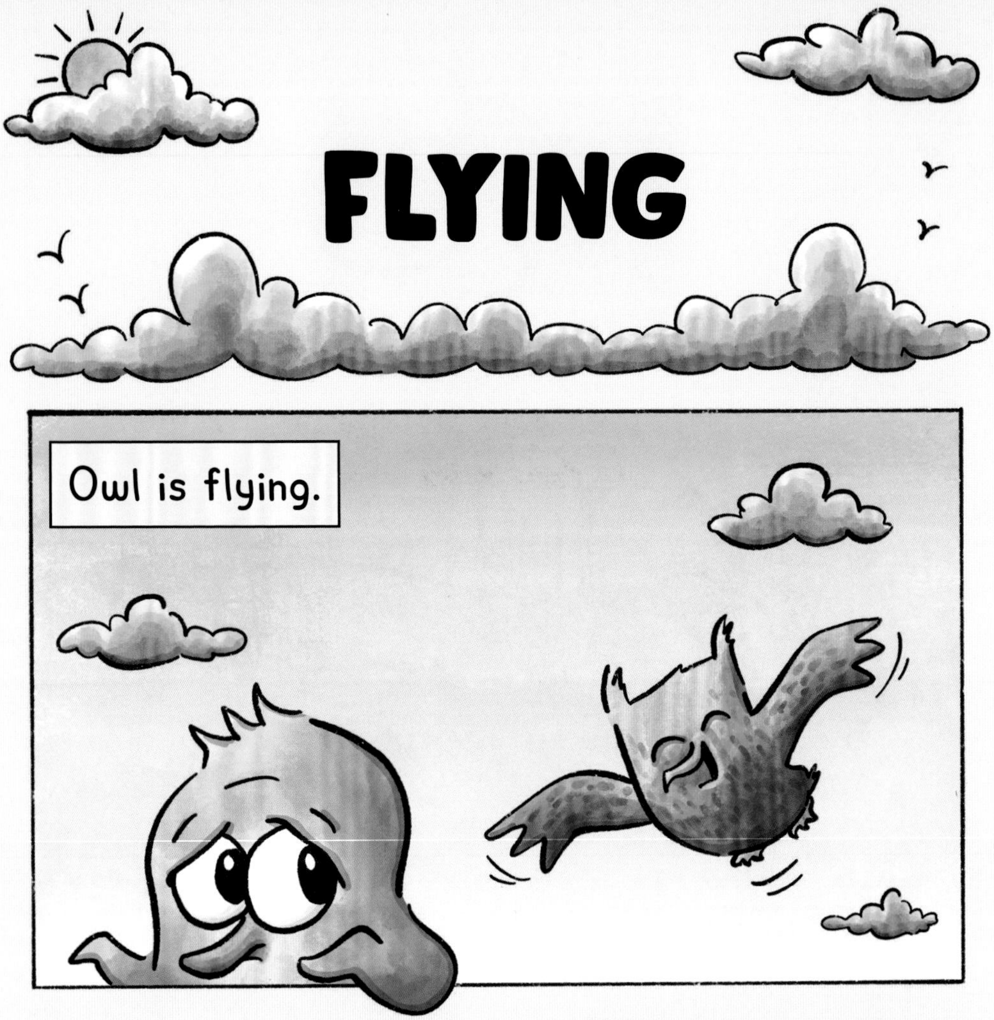
Owl is flying.

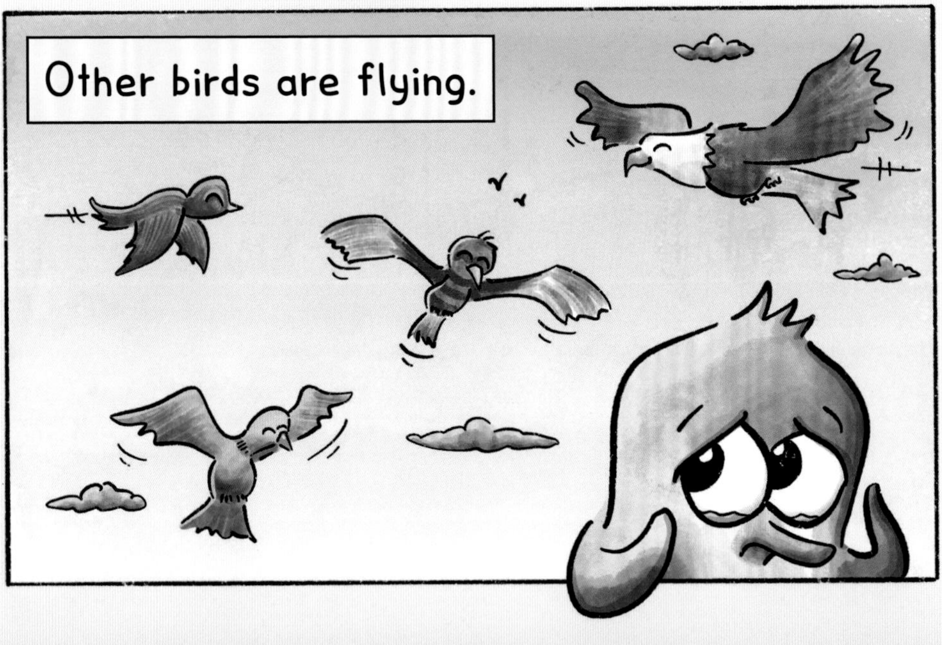
Other birds are flying.

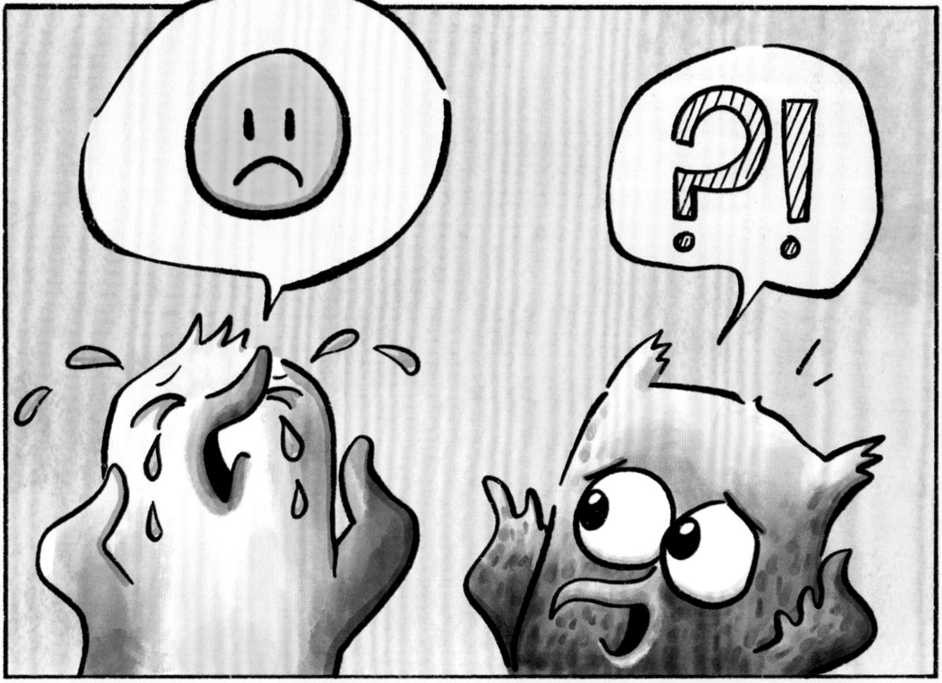
?!

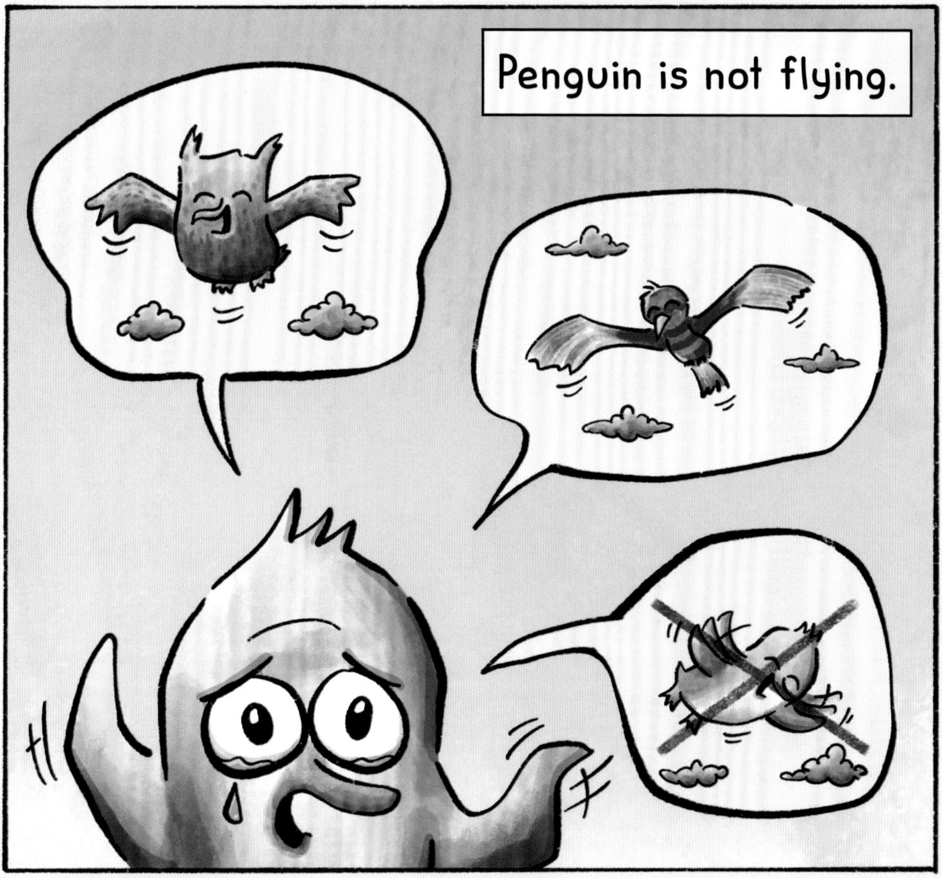
Penguin is not flying.

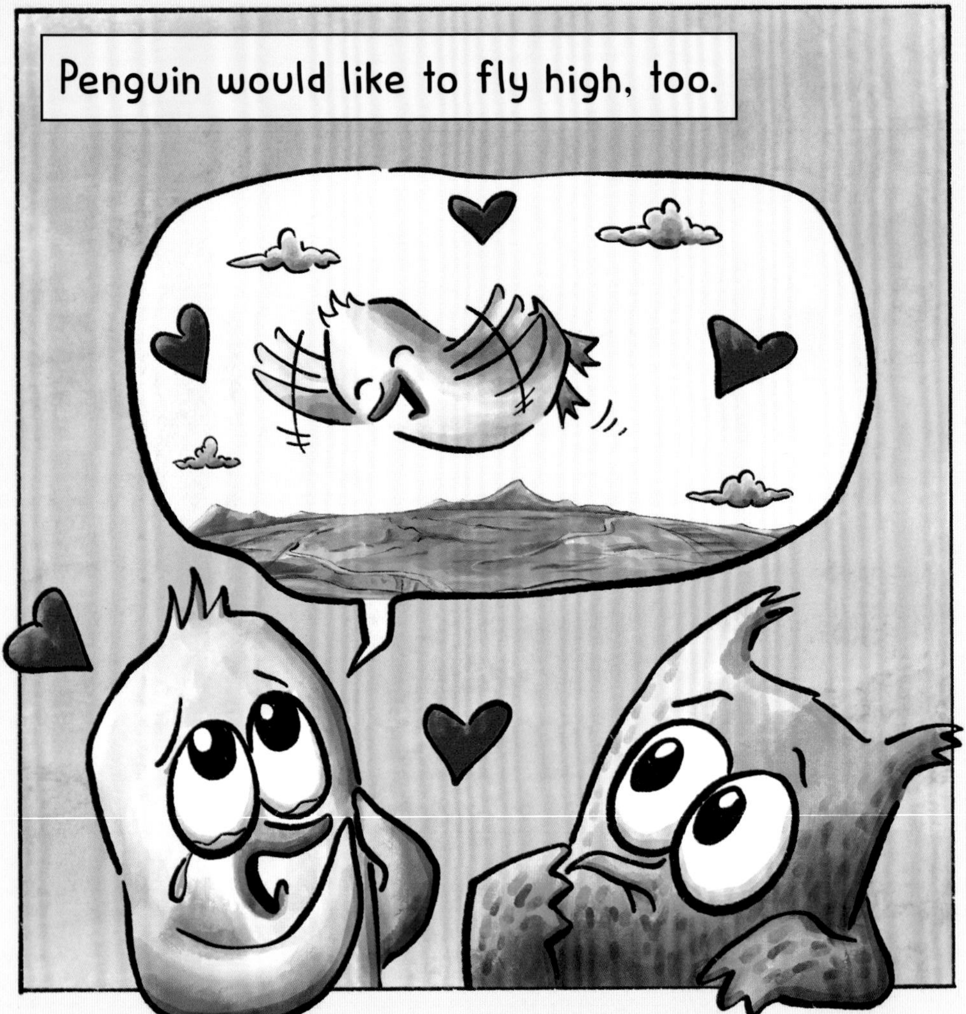
Penguin would like to fly high, too.

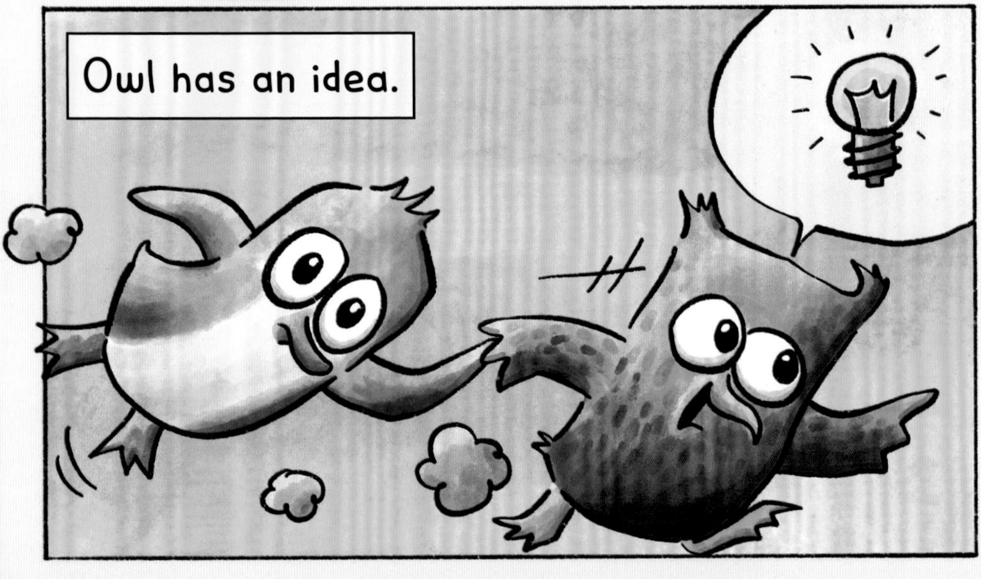
Owl has an idea.

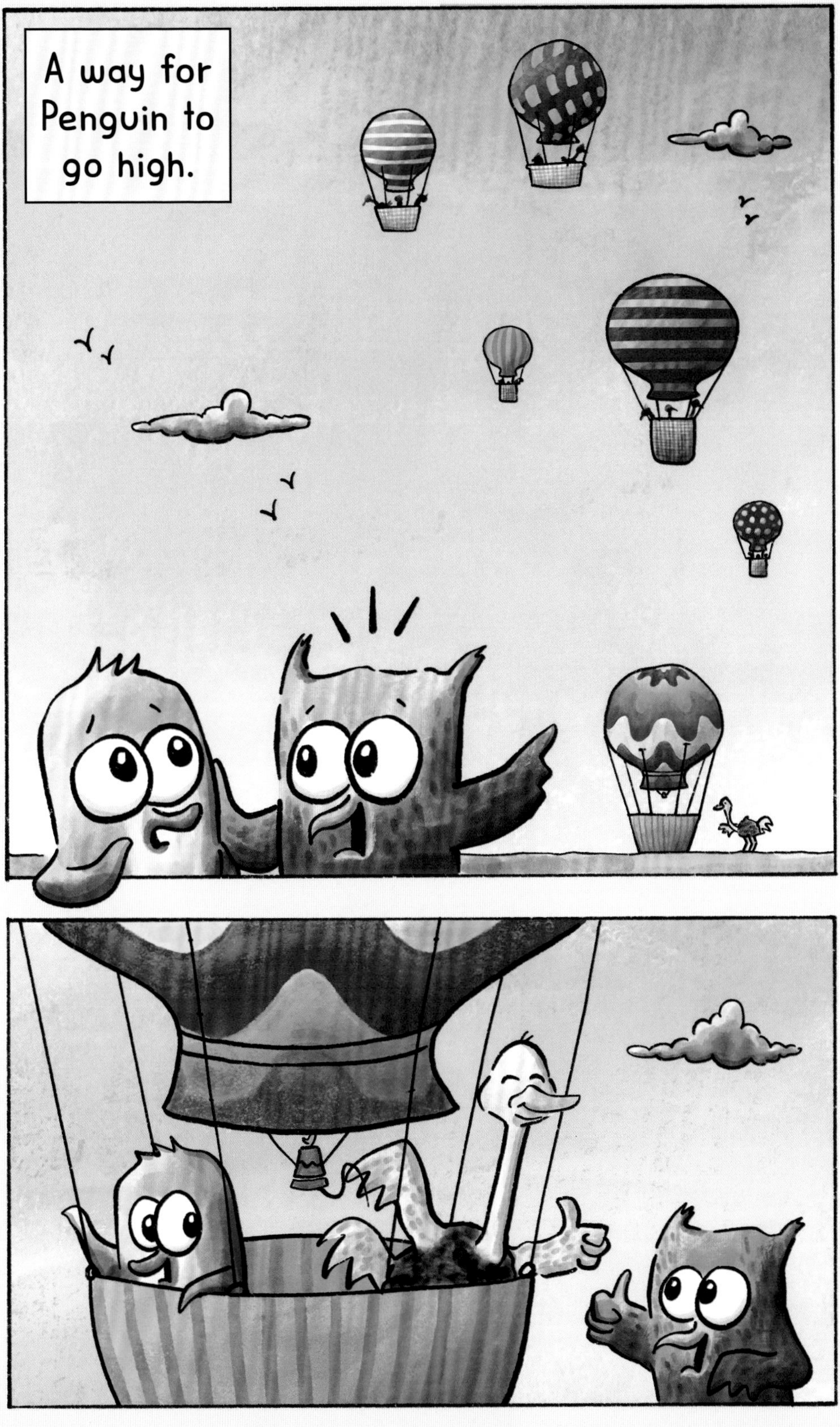
A way for Penguin to go high.

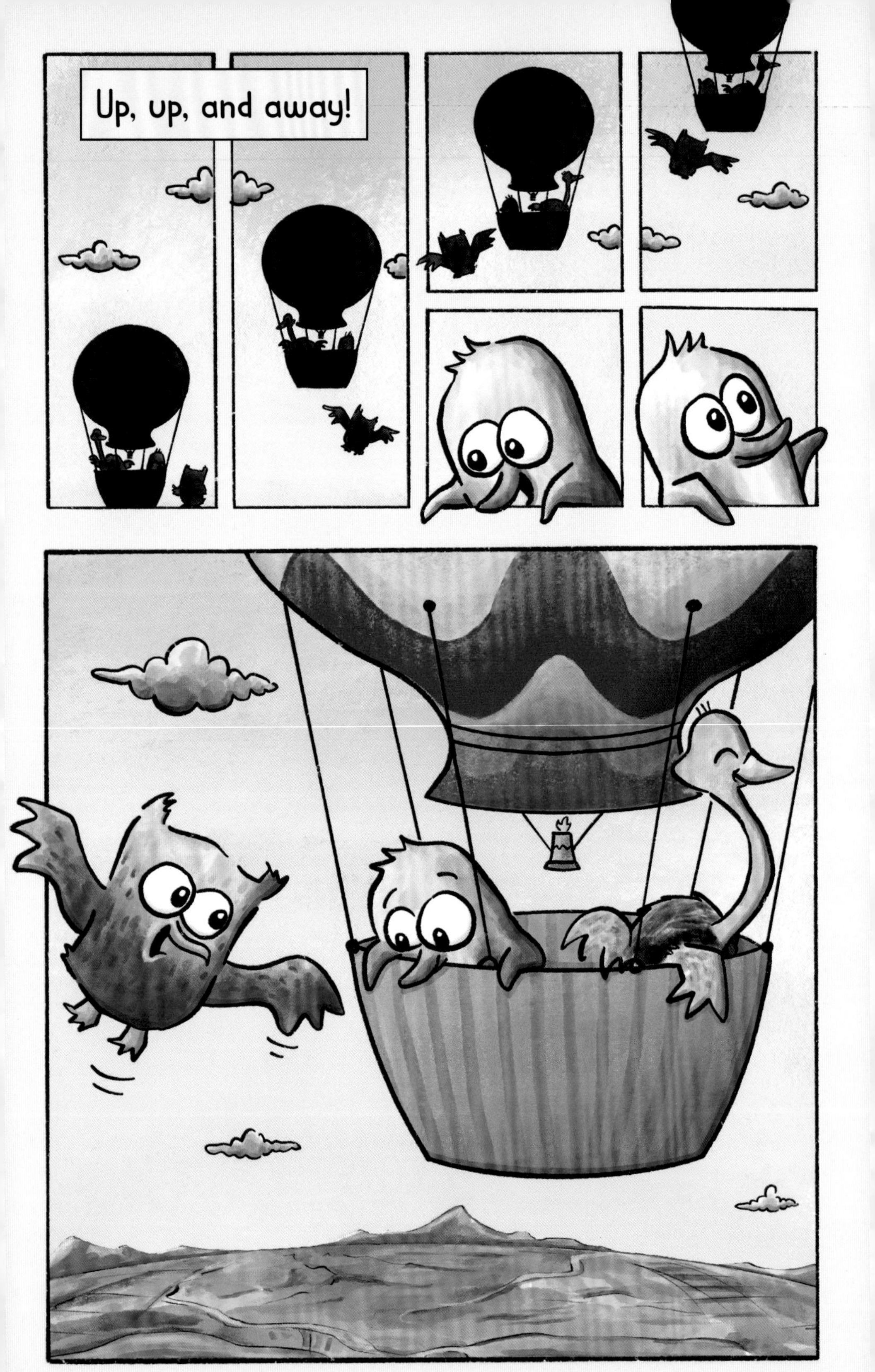
Up, up, and away!

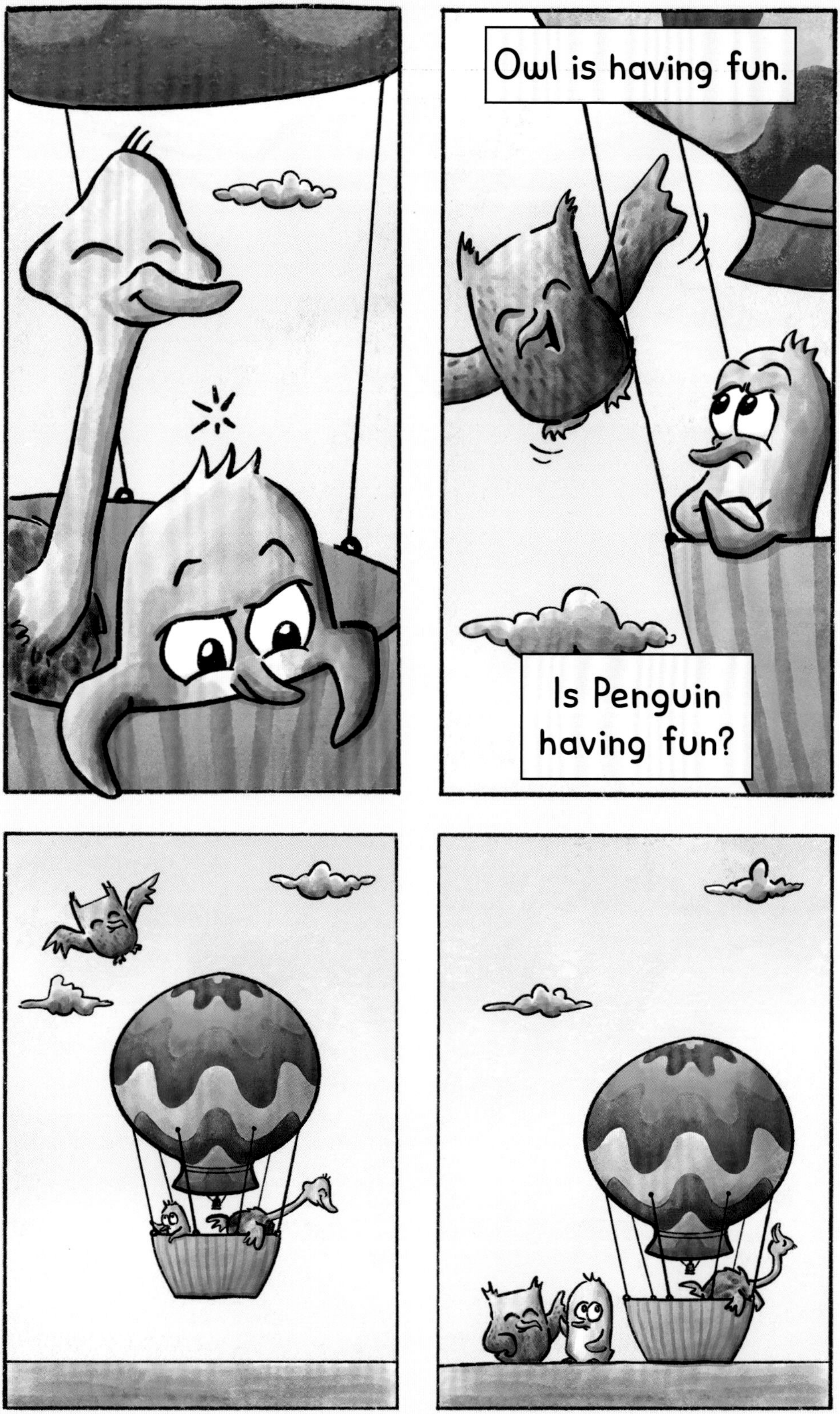
Owl is having fun.
Is Penguin having fun?

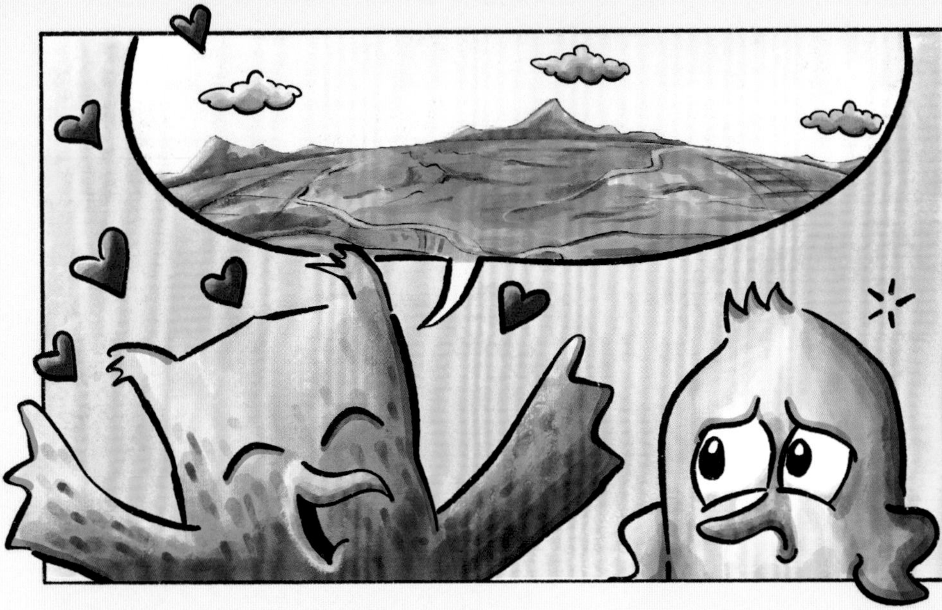

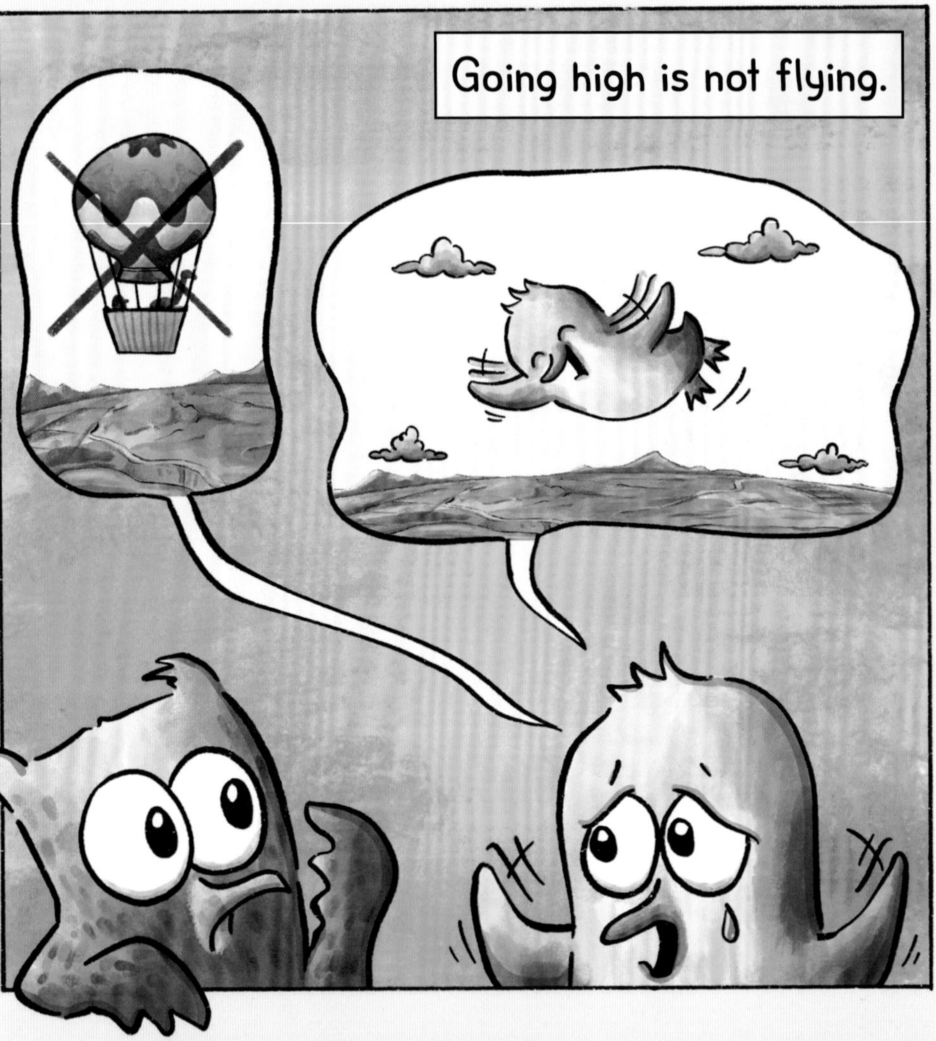
Going high is not flying.

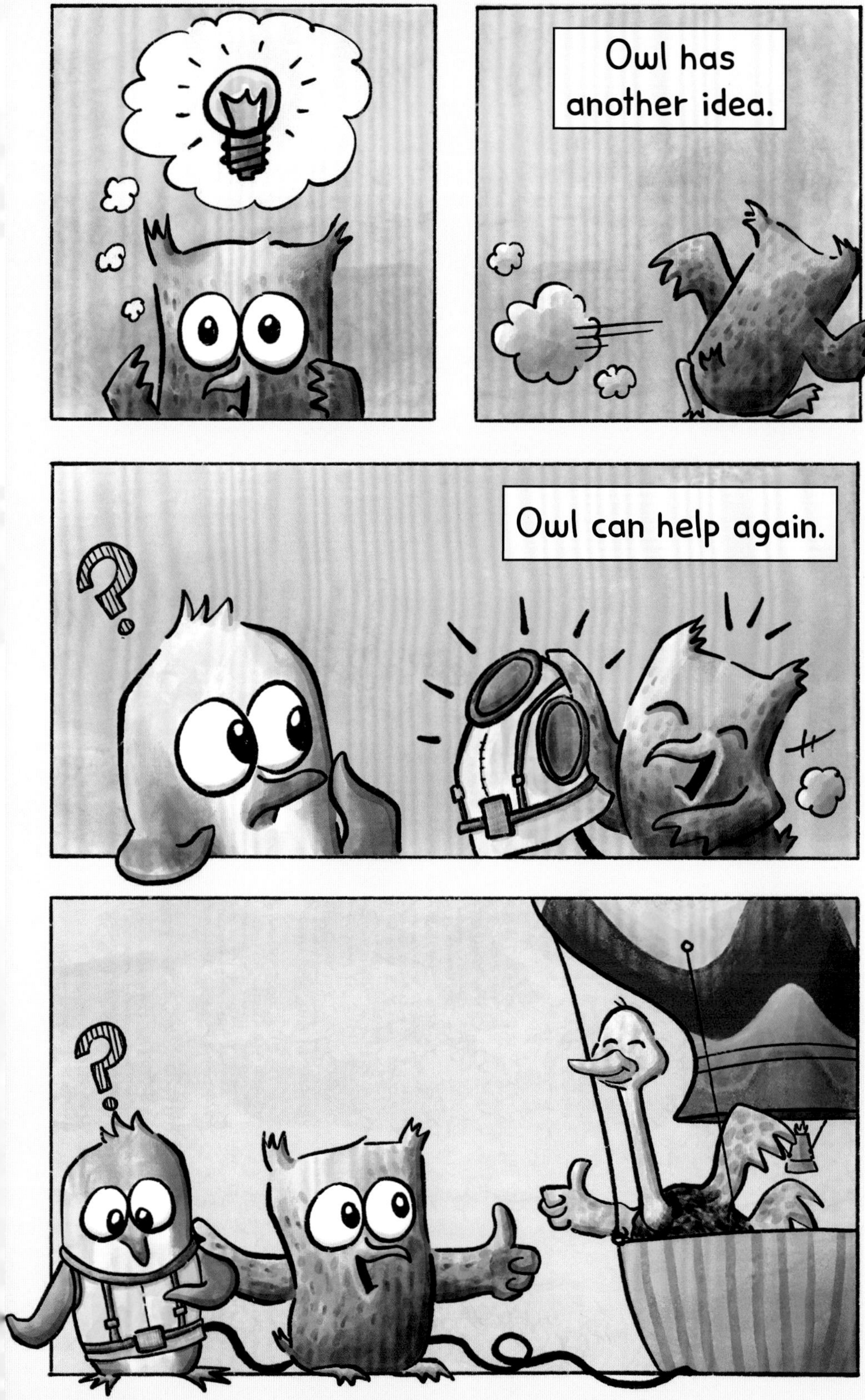
Owl has another idea.
Owl can help again.

Owl and Penguin
are flying.

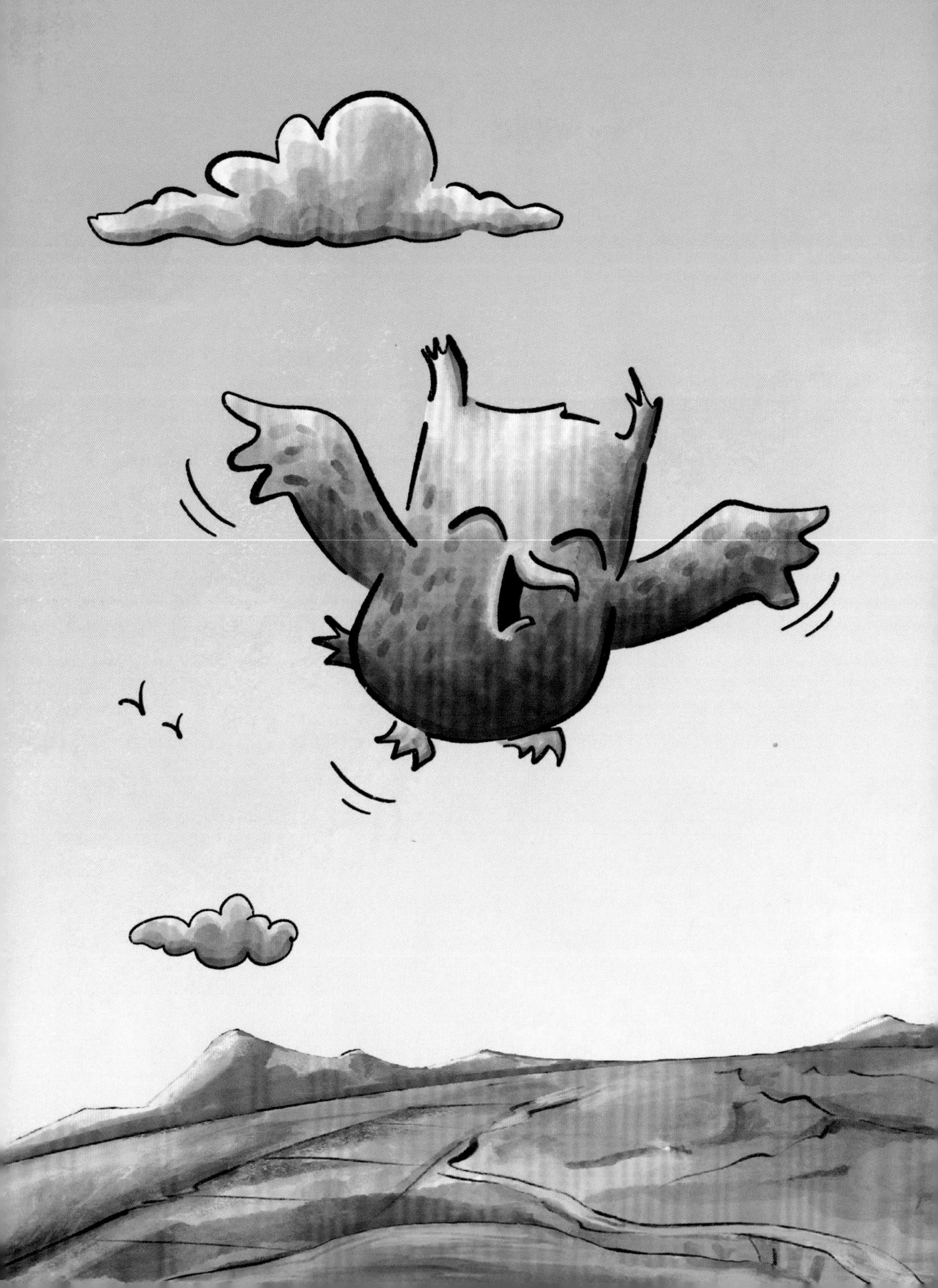

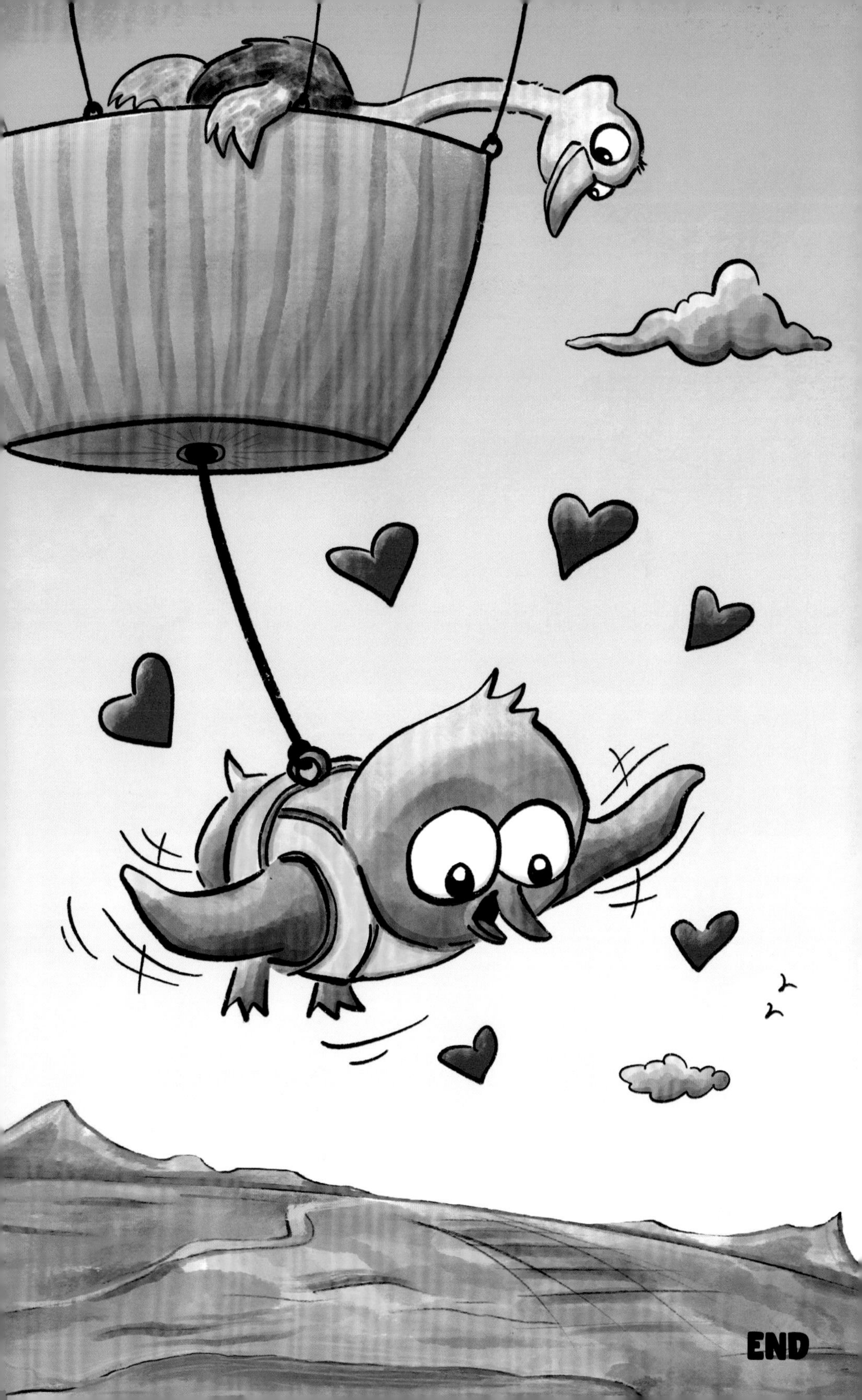
END

SPLISH-SPLASH

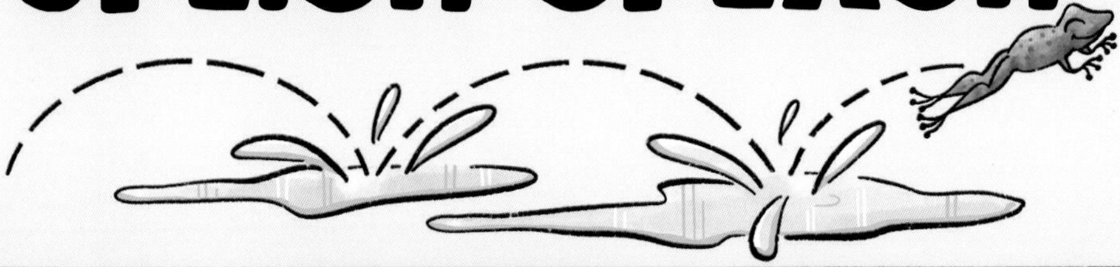

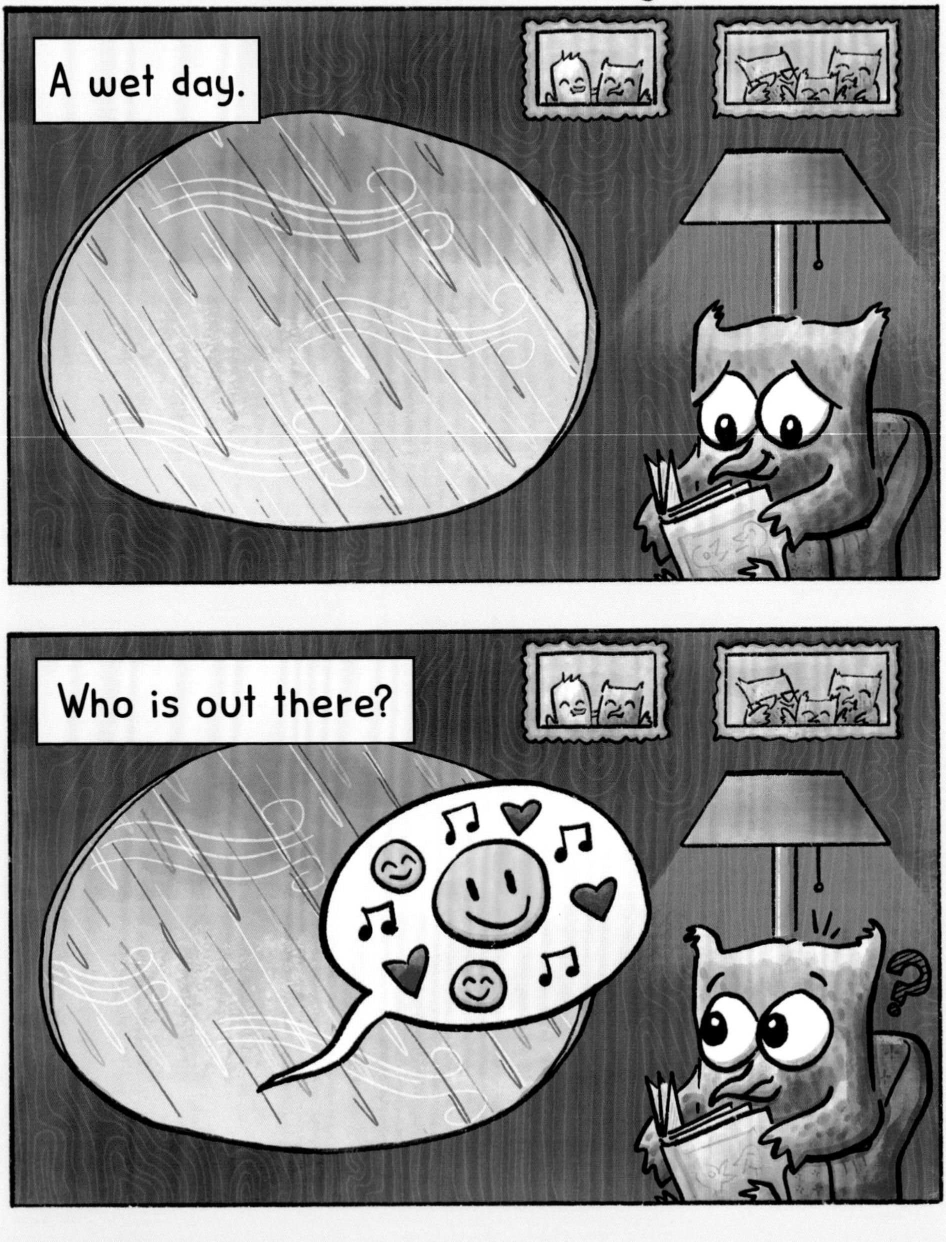
A wet day.
Who is out there?

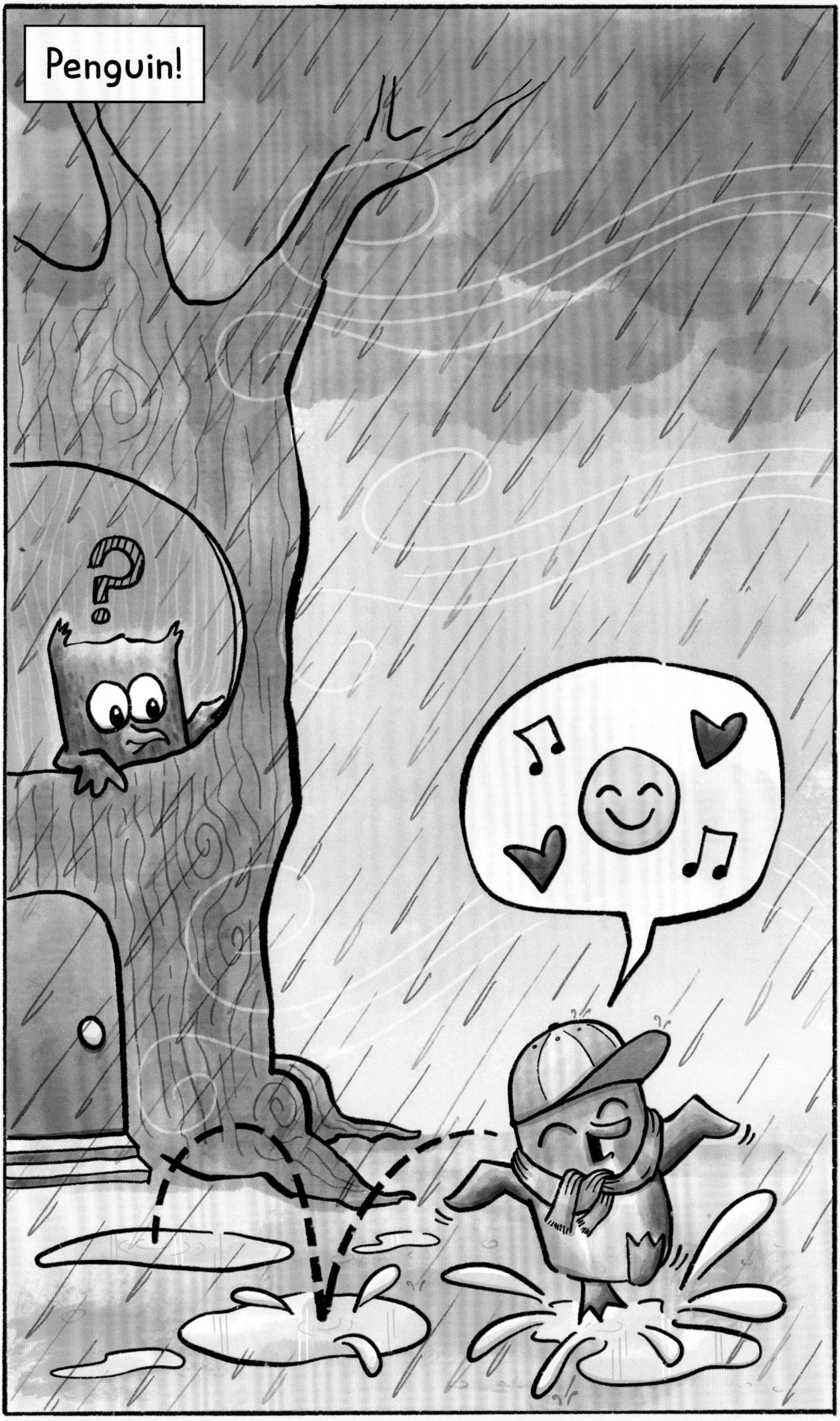
Penguin!

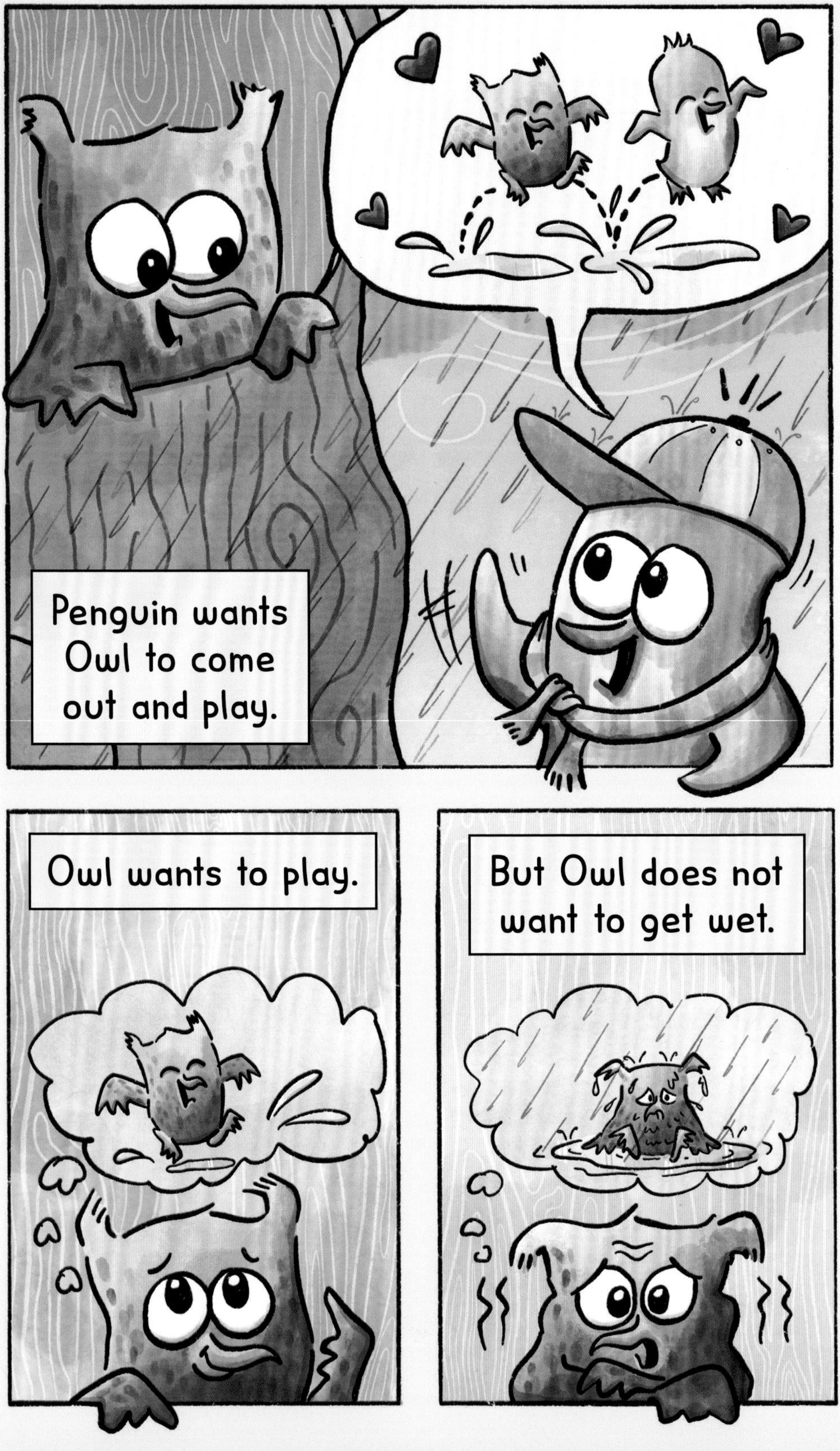
Penguin wants Owl to come out and play.
Owl wants to play.
But Owl does not want to get wet.

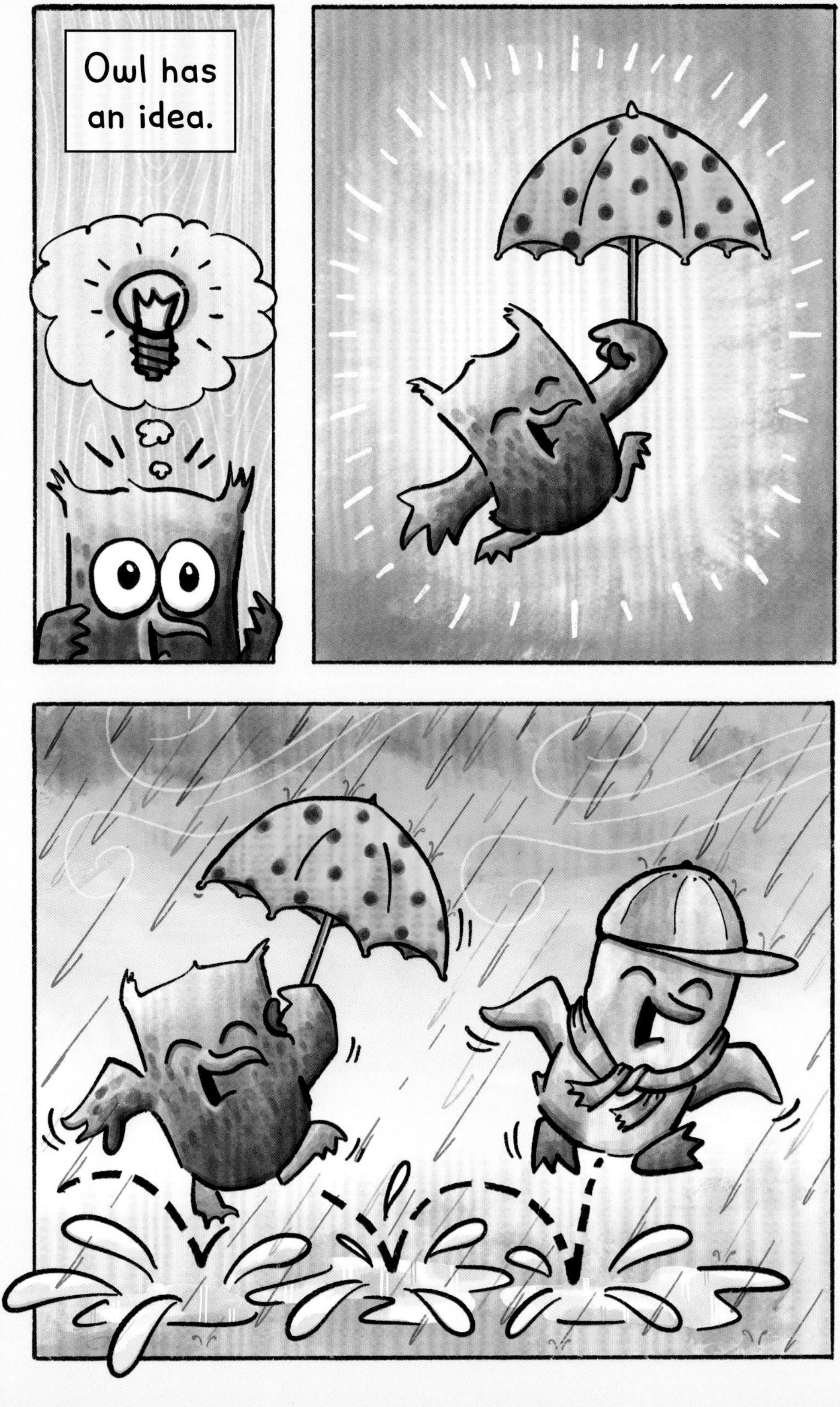
Owl has an idea.

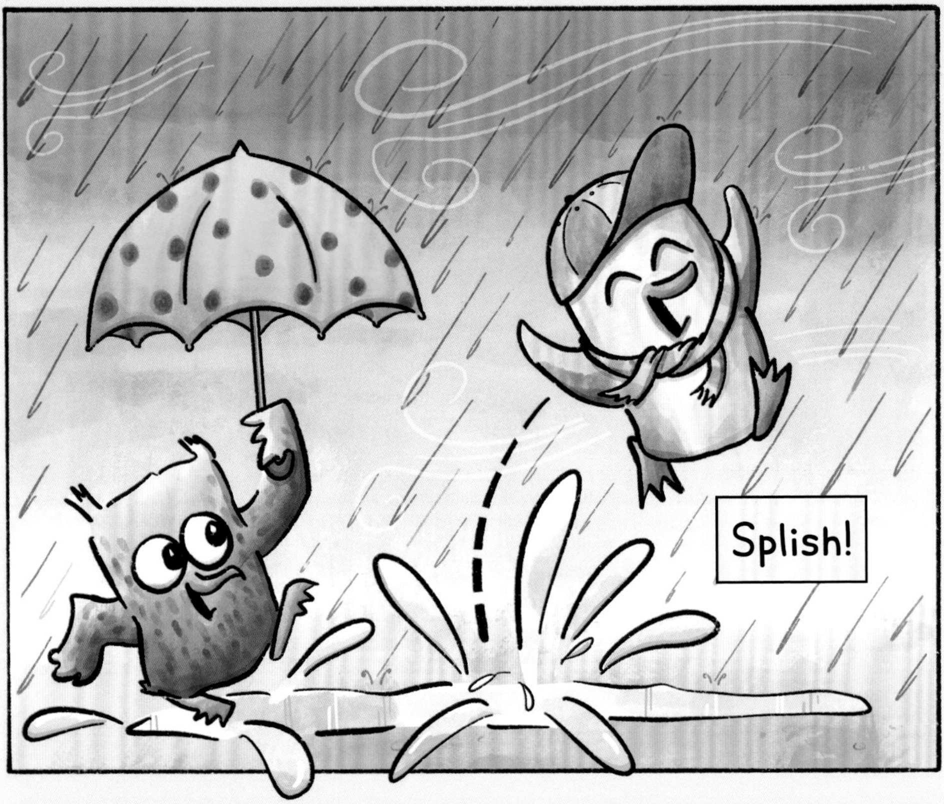
Splish!

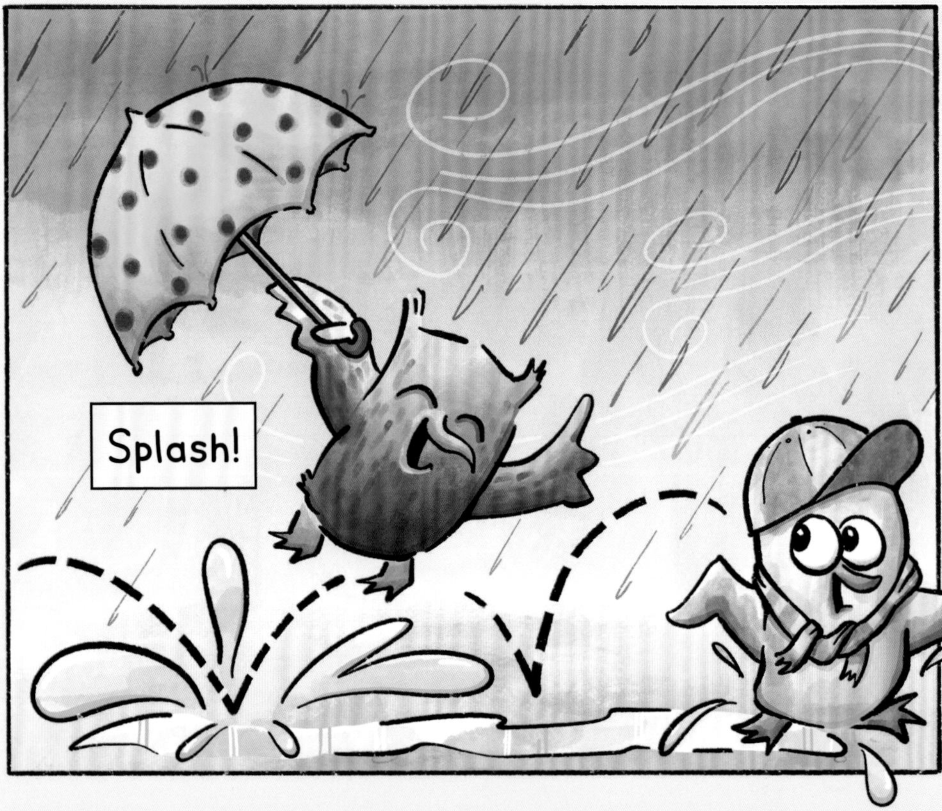
Splash!

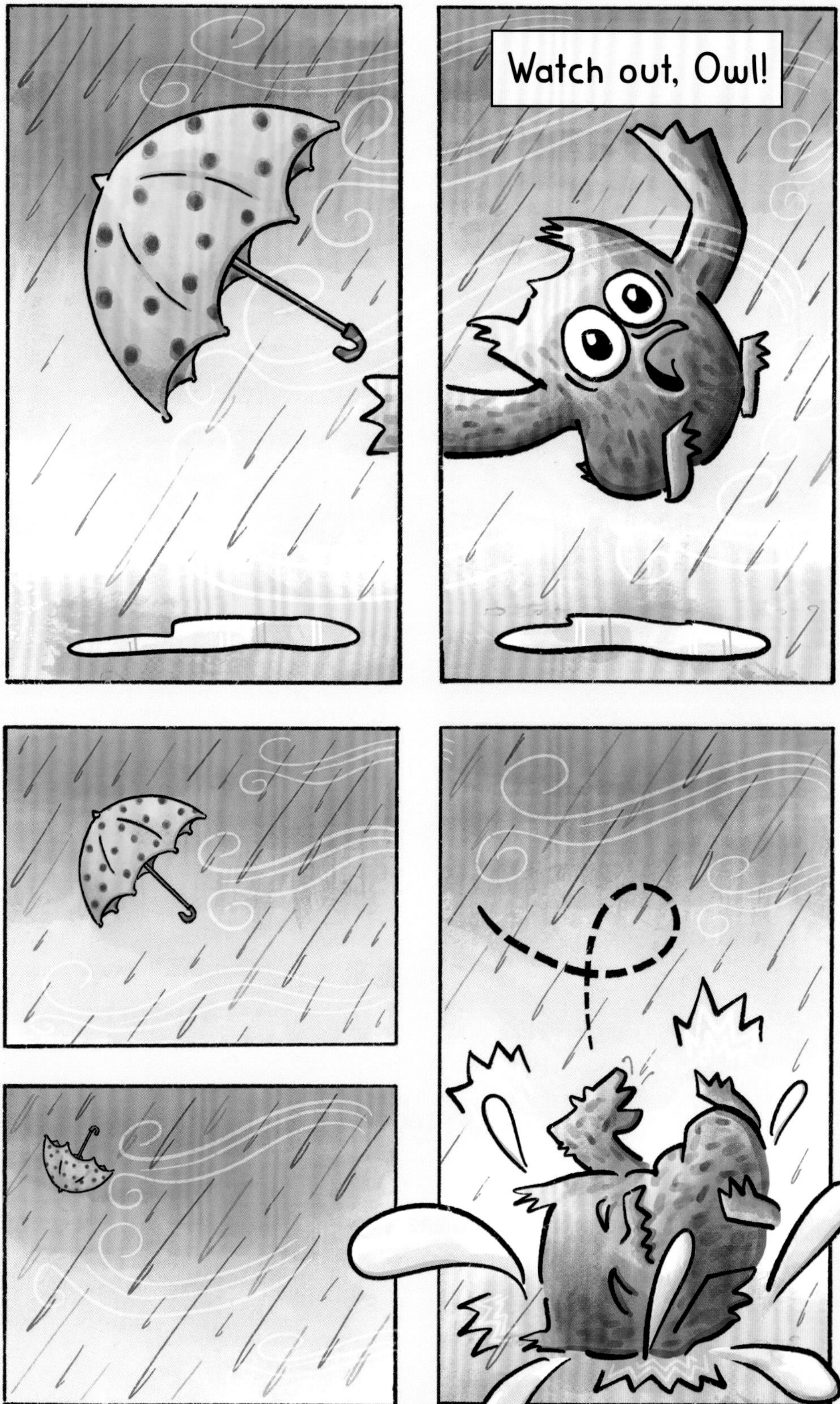
Watch out, Owl!

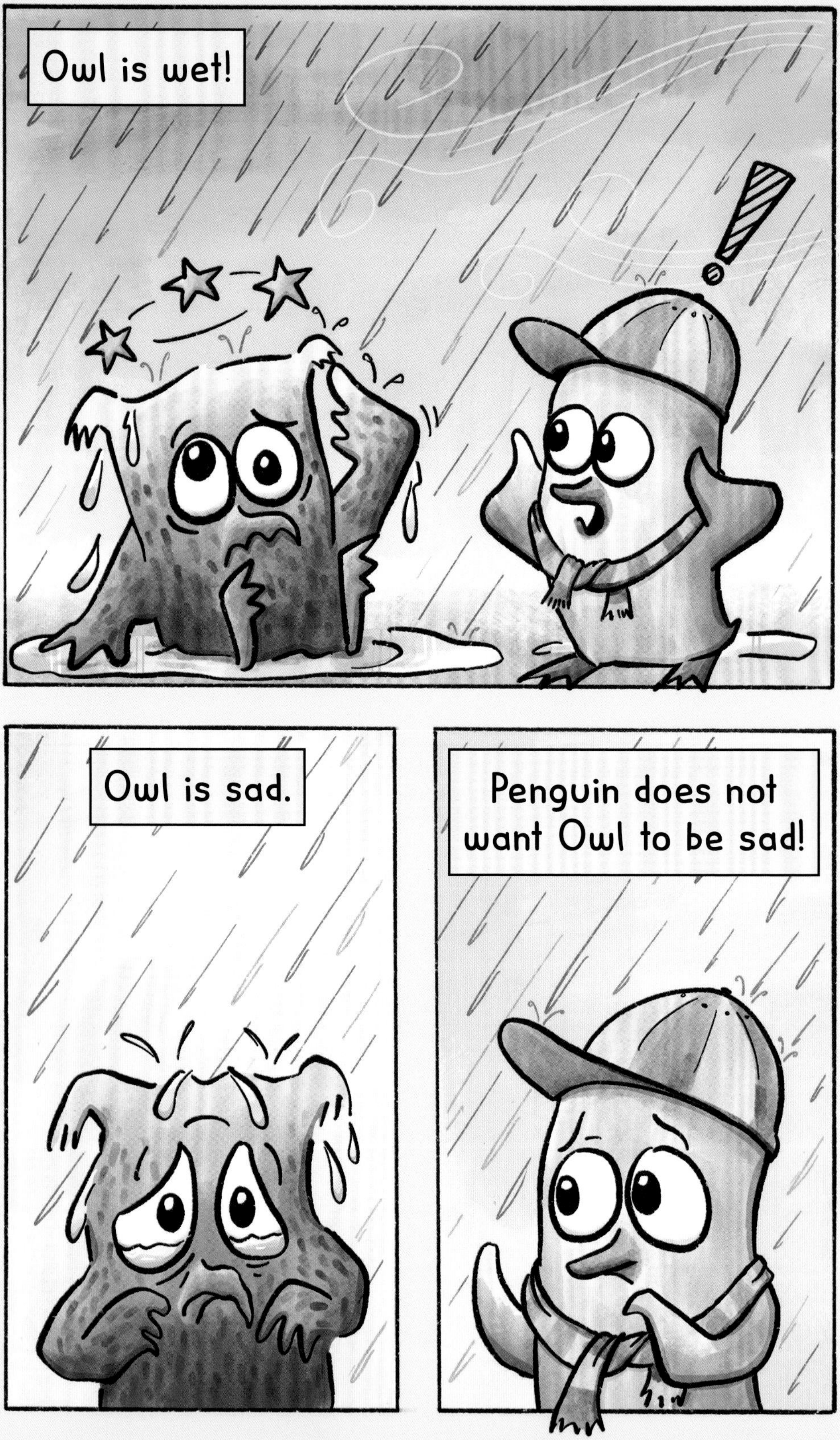
Owl is wet!
Owl is sad.
Penguin does not want Owl to be sad!

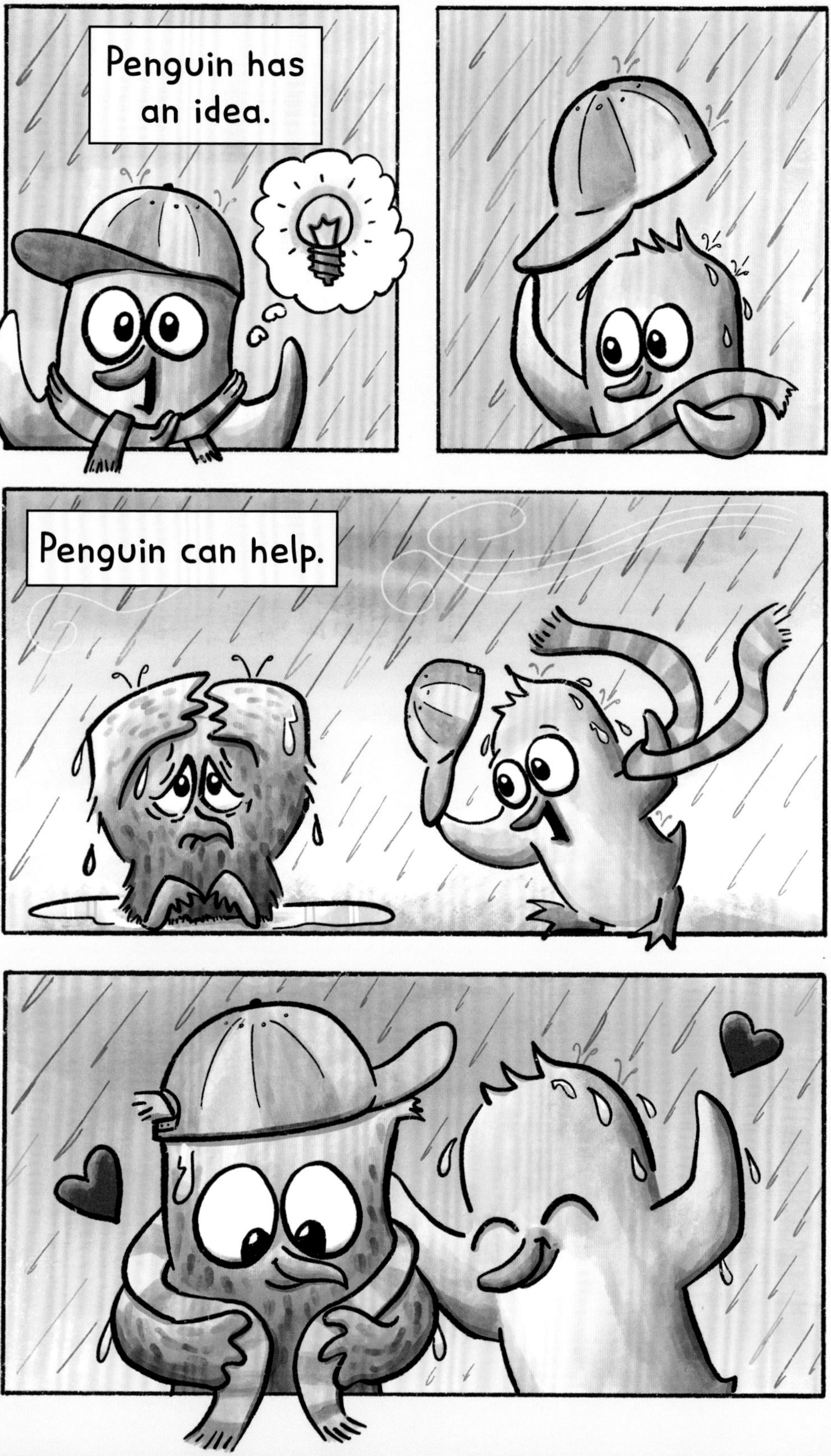
Penguin has an idea.
Penguin can help.

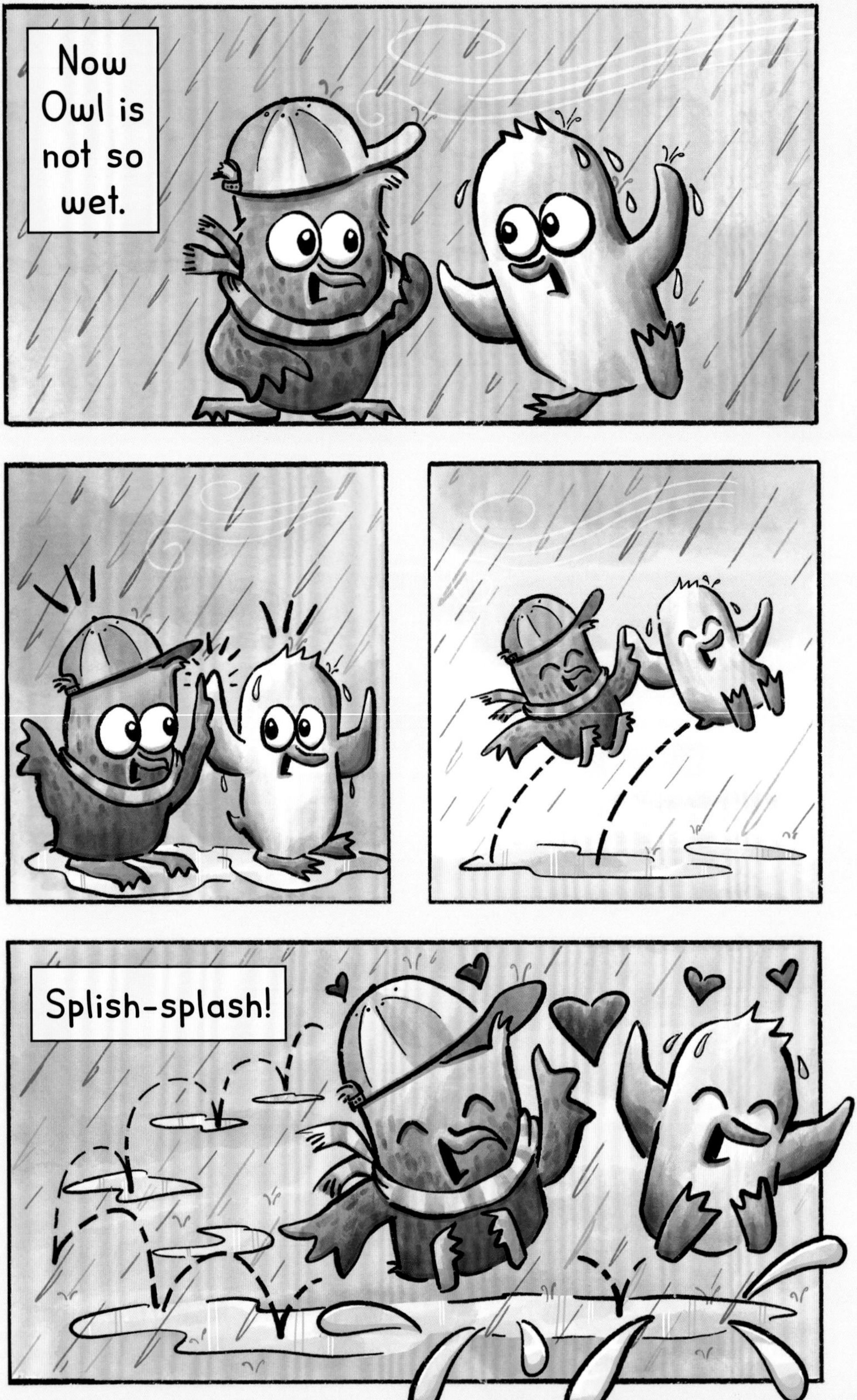
Now Owl is not so wet.
Splish-splash!

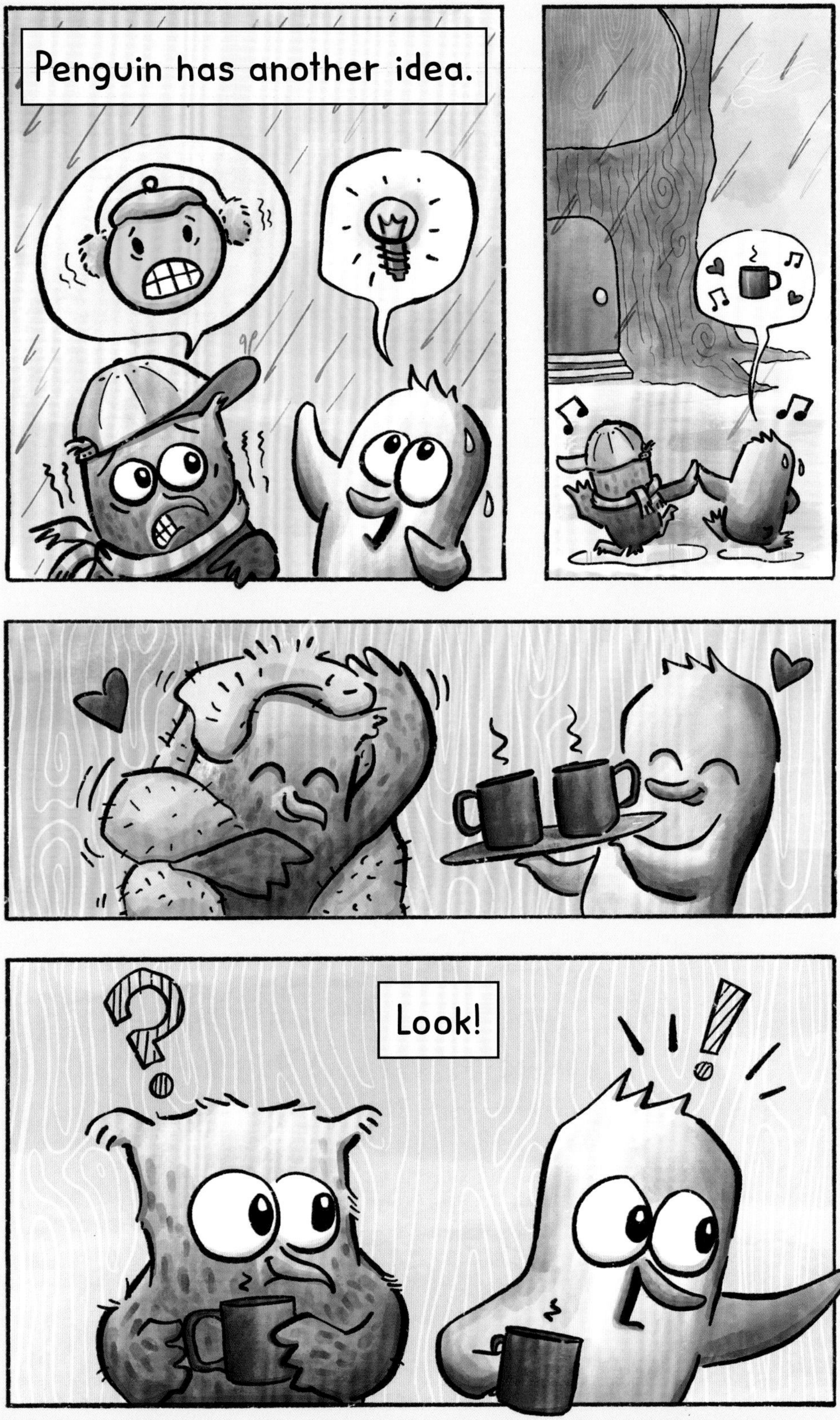
Penguin has another idea.
Look!

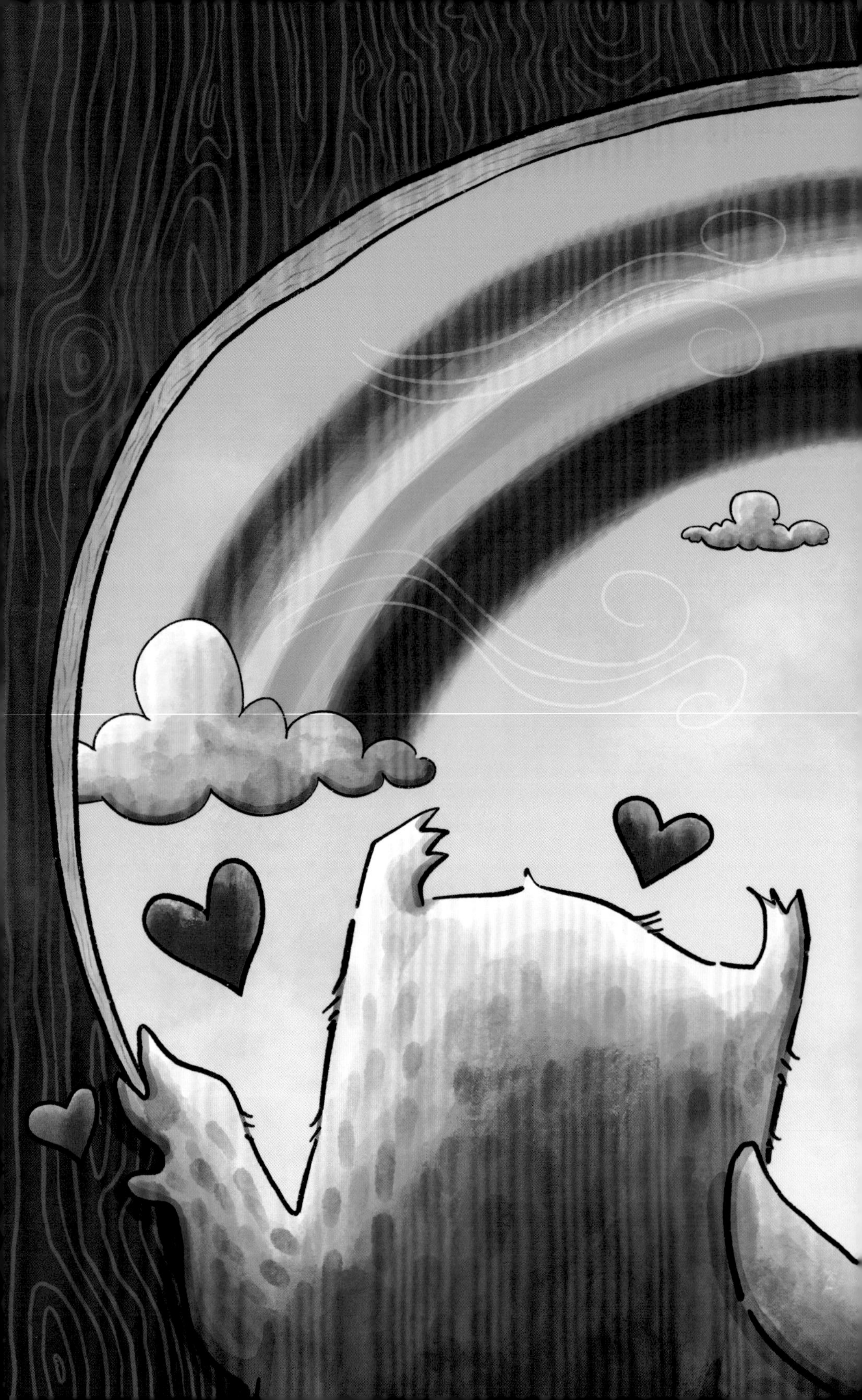

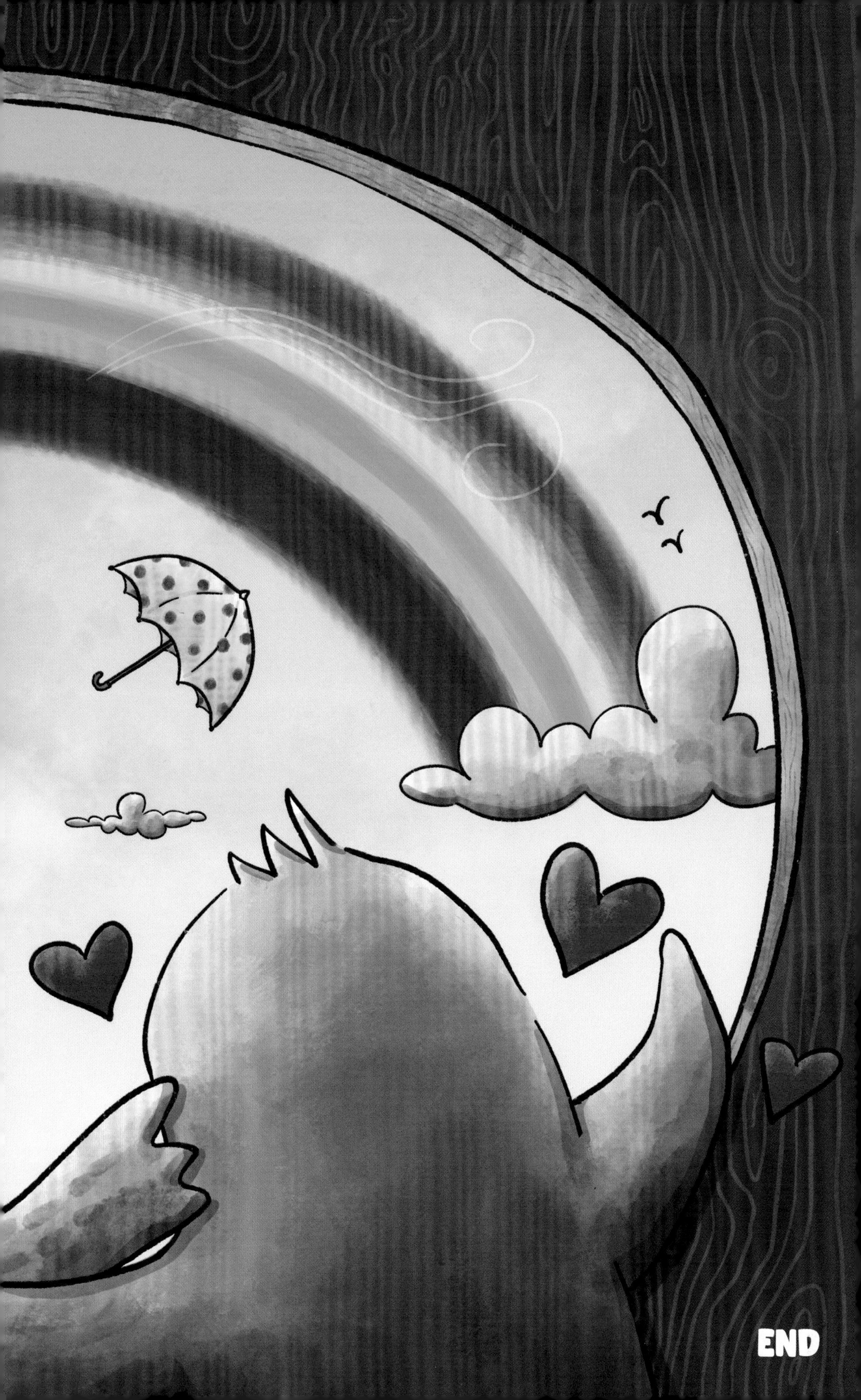
END

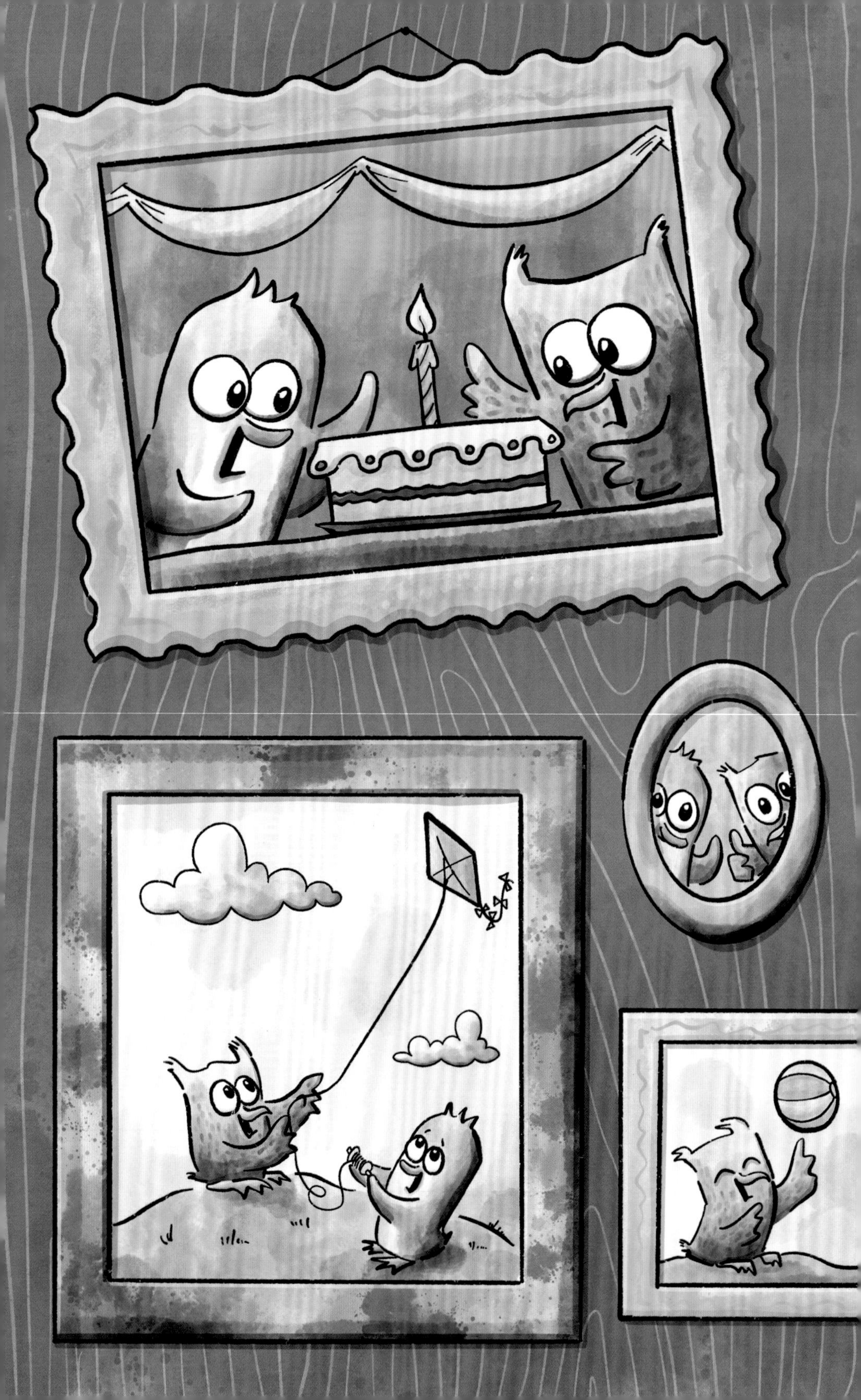